The best writers are part-librarian and part-swashbuckler. At least that seems to be the career path followed by Ian C. Douglas. After a nerdy childhood spent in the company of Tolkien, Lovecraft, and a certain time lord, Ian ran away to see the World. This quest for adventure landed in him countless scrapes, before finding himself teaching English in East Asia. After ten years of hard grammar, he returned to his native England, and graduated with a MA Distinction in Creative Writing. Since then he has written everything from online computer games to apps for children. Several of his stories have won prizes and he was a finalist in the Independent on Sunday's writing competition. Ian is a children's history author and visits schools with bloodcurdling tales of the past. His writing has appeared at the V&A's Toy Museum.

Ian lives near Sherwood Forest with his wife and children. When he's not daydreaming about Martian landscapes, he teaches creative writing and writes theatre reviews. Interests include origami, astronomy and wearing silly hats.

Science Fiction has always been Ian's first love. He is delighted to launch his first sci-fi novel for younger adults as part of the IFWG stable.

Follow Ian at facebook.com/ian.douglas.3994

The Infinity Trap

by
Ian C. Douglas

The Infinity Trap
All Rights Reserved
ISBN-13: 978-0-9923654-1-7
Copyright ©2013 Ian C. Douglas/IFWG Publishing Australia
V1.0

IFWG Publishing Australia
www.ifwgaustralia.com

A big thank you to David Belbin, Stephanie Williams, Megan Taylor and Gerry Huntman. Special thanks to my wonderful wife, Aoy and my sons Zachary and Jesada. And for those who said I'd never become a writer, my undying gratitude. You gave me the biggest motivation.

Part One

Chapter One

The Trans-Tibetan Highway, AD 2259

The tower glinted against the sky. Zeke blinked in the fierce sunlight and searched for a glimpse of the top. But there was no top. The building zoomed up forever.

"I told you already, bro," snapped the fat geeky boy in the next seat. "The Televator's too high. Pack a telescope next time."

He was right, but Zeke needed a distraction from his fears. Perhaps the smell would do it. He breathed in the ripe air and grimaced. After two days of travelling the hover-bus was beginning to remind him of a zoo. The fat boy wrinkled his nose.

"Stinks worse than a gorilla's butt in here."

Zeke tensed up. Had the stranger been reading his thoughts? Some of them could, he knew that. If his lies were discovered now, six months of hopes and planning would be ruined. He focused on the grey Tibetan plateau, but that was as endlessly flat as their destination was high. The painful memory of Heathrow's Terminal Twenty bounced back into his head.

"You're going to be the best Star Mariner ever," his mum said, biting back tears. She didn't want him to go, naturally, but she had no say in the matter. Every child who passed the Exam, everyone onboard the bus, became government property.

She hugged him and walked away, fading quickly into the crowds. She didn't know. Nobody knew. Zeke had faked it through the Exam, the interview and half way across the world. Now the last hurdle waited for him, the Televator, brooding on the horizon like a hangman's scaffold.

They were nearing another roadside restaurant. The driver steered the gleaming bus off the road and into the car park.

"Oh great," the nerd groaned. "More yak burgers, more yak shakes! Any more Tibetan cooking and I'll morph into a yak!"

"Newsflash, yak-boy, you already have!" called a pimply boy from the front.

The others all laughed. The escort, a skinny sour-faced man, threw them a stern look.

"Quieten down folks," he said. "Okay, lunch. Then everyone back on the vehicle in thirty minutes. We've got an interplanetary travel schedule to stick to."

A cold Himalayan draught whistled through the deserted restaurant. As the last stop before the Televator, the place had been decorated in a space theme. Flimsy polystyrene rockets dangled from the ceiling. Tatty posters revelled in long ago glories of space exploration. Astronauts planted flags on the lunar surface, constructed space stations and lifted up the colossal Televator.

Zeke bought a Full Moon Pizza with Salami Craters and scanned for an empty chair. Most of the others were sat by the window, chattering like monkeys. A few looked in his direction but he quickly turned away. They seemed a smug lot, with their luxury ski-suits and designer boots. His cheeks burned as he glanced down at his second-hand coat. *No doubt they all had successful fathers*, he thought enviously. Zeke longed for a dad. An unsuccessful one would do just fine.

He spied the geek alone in a corner. The boy was gulping down Saturn Rings, really onions rings, and playing with a Laserlight Mini-Deluxe. The small console had transformed the tabletop into a holographic battlefield. Tiny glowing commandoes hunted among the dirty plates for a disgustingly ugly alien. Zeke recognised the holo-game as *Blood Guzzler III,* not due in the stores until summer. This geek was one very rich kid.

"Hey, I love that game," Zeke said in his coolest voice.

The boy said nothing, scowling intensely at his miniature figures.

Zeke persevered, flicking the nearest foam rocket. "These models are, um, neat."

"Neat! Is that a way for saying cheap, tacky garbage where you come from?"

"I guess so," he said quickly. "My name's Zeke Hailey, from—"

"London. Your accent's a giveaway."

"Where are you—?"

"Lakeville, outside Toronto."

"Sorry, never heard of it," Zeke confessed, taking the adjacent seat.

"No sweat, bro. It's in the dictionary under dead-end. A burger joint, a pizza place and you're done."

An awkward pause filled the air as they weighed each other up. The fat boy resembled a frog in a blond wig. His hair was long and greasy, his eyes too far apart, and his nose flat.

Zeke blushed as the nerd returned the stare. He awkwardly combed his fingers through his unruly blue hair.

"Oh, my hair?" he added with a half-hearted laugh. "Mum always says a cartridge of nano-dye fell on my head as a baby. Turned me bluer than a parrot!"

The geek didn't return the laugh. Instead he searched deeper, into Zeke's dark burning eyes and crooked smile, as if something was missing. Zeke shifted uncomfortably on the hard seat. He wondered if the boy could sense his secret.

At that moment the alien leapt out from behind a pepper pot and devoured a shrieking hologram soldier. The frog-boy stretched out his hand.

"Scuff Barnum."

They shook manfully.

"So what was your score?" Scuff asked, an inevitable question. It was thanks to the ESP exam that they were going to Mars. The letters stood for 'extrasensory perception' and every fifteen year old on the planet sat the exam. And every fifteen year old who passed was onboard the rather small coach.

Zeke blushed. For all his boldness Zeke was a lousy liar.

"D-Doesn't matter. H-How about you?" he stammered.

"I'm not telling if you won't," Scuff barked. He shoved back the table and moved away.

Dusk was falling as they neared the Televator. The unending pillar caught the sunset in a blaze of orange and purple. Zeke strained his eyes, trying again to catch the vanishing point. He marvelled at its height.

"How come it doesn't collapse?" he asked Scuff, who was still sulking beside him.

The geek glared and said nothing. Zeke turned his attention to the plasma screen in the back of the next seat. He tapped in his question and text appeared.

Carbon nano-tubes, the strongest and stiffest material on Earth, are welded together molecule by molecule creating a strength greater than diamonds—

"Any time now!" the escort proclaimed, distracting Zeke from the screen.

A hush filled the coach as the Televator erupted into light. A million photon lamps raced up, into the twilight, glittering like a cosmic Christmas tree.

The sobbing of a little girl broke the silence. Zeke got up and stumbled through the darkness towards the sound. It was one of the Chinese students, a tiny girl with a short bob of hair and a face as round as the Moon.

He sat down beside her.

"They say space travel is as safe as crossing the road," he said, taking her hand.

"Supposing we die up there? My daddy told me there's no air on Mars," she replied in perfect English.

"No, no, that was in the past. There's plenty of air now, at least where we're going."

The girl pointed to a battered old teddy bear beside her.

"Mr Raffles is homesick."

"Aren't we all? I keep thinking about my mum."

The girl's tearful expression gave way to a puzzled frown.

"What about your daddy?"

Zeke gritted his teeth. She'd hit a raw nerve. He was cheating his way into the greatest school in the Solar System for the gravest of reasons.

"My dad's missing."

Ian C Douglas

Chapter Two

The Televator

At midnight the students spilled out of the departure lounge into the cold crisp night. The impossibly huge Televator loomed across the tarmac. Zeke's head swam from the vastness of it all.

"Now I know how an ant feels looking up at a skyscraper," he groaned.

Pin-mei Liang, the little girl from the bus, clung tightly to Zeke's hand. She came from Shanghai and was only eleven years old.

"I'm going to miss school, won't you?" she giggled.

"Aren't you a bit young to be going to Mars?" Zeke said. He felt very grown-up next to her.
Her face dimmed.

"My grades were so high I sat my exams early. I never thought in a million light years I'd pass."

"How did your parents take it?"

The girl swallowed a lump in her throat.

"They told me to be brave. That they were so proud of me."

New tears were forming. Zeke squeezed her hand and she forced a huge grin.

"They said it was an honour to study at the Chasm."

The Chasm! Zeke's heart pumped faster at the sound of that word. The Ophir Chasma Academy for Psychic Endeavour was the name in full, but the media had shortened that mouthful to the Chasm. It was a legend, a dream, an aspiration. Those who graduated from its Martian classrooms made it into the Mariners Institute and became instant celebrities. For a brief time their faces adorned holomags and plasma-screens worldwide in a celebration of their bravery. Then they vanished into deep space, at the helm of a colony ship. The fact no ship had so far returned was no cause for concern, said the politicians. The colonists were too busy building new worlds to cross the galaxy for a social call.

But to get to the Chasm the new intake first had to escape gravity.

Around the base of the Televator sat a donut–shaped cabin large enough for a hundred passengers. A fat uniformed woman emerged through the open door and ushered in the teenagers. The digital badge on her breast read, *Stella Gates, Space Stewardess-in-Chief.* She reeked of garlic and coffee.

"Zeke Hailey, Mr," she remarked, collecting his boarding chip. She ran a disdainful eye over his blue locks. "No running in the aisles. No backchat either or you'll find yourself dangling from the safety exit like a conker on a string. A very cold dead conker. Do I make myself clear?"

"Per-fect-ly," Zeke replied, gagging on a cloud of bad breath.

"Good, and have a pleasant flight."

"Can I stay with you?" Pin-Mei asked, once they were inside.

Zeke nodded, putting on a brave smile.

As they claimed the nearest seats, Scuff stomped past, hunting for a spare place. He saw Zeke, muttered something grumpy-sounding and turned away. He glanced back to check they were still watching him.

"Come and join us," Zeke ventured.

Scuff coloured slightly but accepted the invitation.

"About lunchtime, bro, sorry I blew my stack. Never been into space before and I'm as edgy as a man with a beehive down his pants."

"Um, I know what you mean, I think," Zeke replied, trying hard not to think about bees and underwear.

"Your exam score is your business," Scuff said in an awed voice. "Guess you're a top ten percenter, bro!"

Zeke lowered his head. *If only Scuff knew the truth*, he thought guiltily.

Stella Gates cleared her throat. A couple of youngsters at the front went a very pale green.

"Boys and girls, soon we will be travelling up one of the greatest wonders in the world. The Televator! For the scientifically minded let me explain this miracle. A magnet the size of a small city lies buried beneath our feet. This is called the Base Magnet and acts as a catapult."

"Must have one hell of a rubber sling!" jeered a pimply boy. It was the same joker who had called Scuff a yak-boy. Stella raised a haughty eyebrow.

"No, darling, an electromagnetic catapult. Tremendous magnetic energy shoots up inside the tower. The Cruiser is divided into two rings. The inner ring houses our magnetic dynamo, while the outer ring serves as the passenger deck. Once the inner ring starts rotating, it creates a magnetic field."

Scuff raised his hand. "Which is the same as the Base Magnet."

A volley of sneers passed through the compartment.

"Ah, I see we have a scholar among us," Stella beamed. "Opposites attract but alike repel. It's the same principle."

"All that spinning will make us throw up!" the pimply boy protested.

"The passenger deck remains constant," Gates explained through a strained smile. "And it's a lot cheaper and safer than those primitive rockets our great-grandfathers travelled in. About as sophisticated as sitting on a ton of dynamite and lighting the fuse. No wonder they were always blowing up midair."

At that moment a violent banging interrupted Stella's speech. Someone was trying to get in. Hastily she threw open the airlock.

An enormous man waved his tickets at the flight attendant.

"Entrance woman, I demand entrance!"

The man stormed inside carrying a crocodile-skin suitcase. He was unusually tall with the large flaring nostrils of a horse. His hair flowed in grey oily curls. His black coat billowed around him like a vampire's cape. He cast the youngsters an icy glare.

"These are tomorrow's heroes? Still wetting their panties if you ask me."

His eyes met Zeke's and a cold tingle danced somersaults down Zeke's spine.

"Straight on for First Class," Stella Gates indicated with a wave.

"Yes, yes, I've done this journey countless times," the tall man hissed, and strode off.

Scuff whistled softly.

"You do know who that is?"

Zeke and Pin-Mei shook heads.

He rolled his eyes.

"Wow, bro, don't they have newscasts in merry old England? That was Professor Tiberius Magma, the world famous archaeologist. The first man to explore the Earth's core and discover the lost ruins of Atlantis. Maybe he's off to the Big Pumpkin too?"

"Where?" Zeke and Pin-mei asked at the same time.

"Mars of course! It's orange and round! Like a pumpkin," Scuff barked at them. "Sheesh, I'm wasted on you two!"

"But why would an archaeologist be going to Mars?" Zeke asked.

"To dig up more ruins?" Pin-mei suggested.

Scuff rolled his eyes again.

"There *aren't* any ruins on Mars. Nobody ever lived there before Mankind. Most of its still a dead planet. Outside Mariner's Valley."

"Mariners Valley?" Pin-mei said, rubbing her button nose.

"Where the school is," Scuff snapped. "Biggest canyon in the Solar System."

The cabin lights dimmed. An uneasy silence settled on the passengers. Pin-mei glanced nervously around for something to distract her. She focused on Zeke's head.

"Why is your hair so blue?" she asked in a trembling voice.

Zeke managed a sympathetic smile.

"Mum always says a cartridge of nano-dye dropped on my head as a baby."

"Oh, how awful!" the Chinese girl cried.

Zeke was about to explain it was a joke and blue hair was a family trait when the engines started whirring.

"Buckle up!" Stella bellowed across the aisles.

The grinding noise grew louder.

"We're rising!" someone gasped.

Zeke peeped through the nearest porthole. The rooftops of the departure terminal dropped from sight. A dark canvas of stars and vacuum filled up the aperture. The cabin was lifting.

Pin-mei cried again. Scuff grabbed a copy of the in-flight holomag and pretended to read it. Nobody spoke. Only Zeke, of all the travellers, gazed out at the constellations with a smile.

A whole galaxy lay on the other side of the glass. Planets and nebula and red giants and comets and binary stars. Worlds of fire and worlds of ice, all waiting to be discovered. And somewhere, out among all that coldness and radiation, across thousands of light years, he was going to find his father.

Chapter Three

The Upper Stratosphere

"We're going to stop!"

Zeke swivelled in his seat. Sparks of electricity were dancing in Pin-mei's eyes.

"Sheesh!" Scuff exclaimed. "She's a pre-cog."

Zeke had done his research on all of the psychic senses. Pre-cog was short for 'precognition', people who were able to see quick flashes of the future. But that meant—

"We're going to stop!" she wailed again.

"Miss!" Zeke called out.

"Tsk, tsk, what's up with you two?" Stella snapped, hurrying over.

"We're going to stop," Zeke and Pin-mei cried together.

"Nonsense! This vehicle is unstoppable."

At that very moment the grinding noise of the engines died. The Cruiser slowed, hesitated, and dropped a few feet. It stopped with a loud clang.

"We're going to fall!" the pimply boy shrieked, running his hands through his spiky hair.

A voice boomed from the speakers.

"This is your captain speaking. Do not be alarmed. We are experiencing a minor hitch and have come to a temporary stop thirty miles up. Our magnetic brakes activate automatically at times like these. So lay back and relax while we fix this little inconvenience."

Zeke's stomach churned. The tower was swaying.

"Refreshments anyone?" Stella said a little too loudly, and scurried off to find the hover-trolley.

Pin-mei's eyes had returned to a healthier shade, but she hadn't finished.

"It's in First Class."

"What?" Scuff asked.

"The thing's that stopping us. It's in the bad man's case."

Scuff and Zeke traded baffled looks.

"We'd better tell the attendant," Scuff suggested.

"She won't listen," Zeke replied. They all knew he was right.

"Zeke, why don't you check it out?" Scuff said, biting on his knuckles.

"Me!"

"Well…you're the oldest."

"Um, I suppose, okay."

Zeke unclipped his safety belt and stood up.

"Be careful," Pin-mei said, in an anxious voice.

"Don't worry about me," Zeke replied, in the bravest voice he could muster.

He made a feeble attempt at a carefree grin and began to walk away. After a few steps he hesitated. Scuff had no idea when his birthday was! But it was too late to turn back. Zeke took a deep gulp and walked on.

I t was easier than he expected. The crew were too busy to notice him sidle up to First Class. Professor Magma burst through the doorway as Zeke approached.

"Where's the Captain? This delay is unacceptable!"

He pushed Zeke to one side and stormed off. Zeke checked the coast was clear and slipped inside. He found himself alone in the roomy, leather-bound interior. Luckily the archaeologist was the sole passenger in First Class.

The crocodile case was lying on the Professor's seat. Zeke edged towards it cautiously. He paused. Should he retreat while he had the chance? Magma's magnopad lay adjacent to the case, beeping quietly to itself. He picked it up and pressed the scroll symbol. Words shuffled across the screen. It was an academic report.

Deciphering Martian Runes
By Doctor E. Enki
One: The Significance of Dthoth in Hesperian Mars.
Dthoth was both Alpha and Omega and usually depicted as ؤ

Zeke frowned. Martian runes? He'd never heard of such a thing. His curiosity was hooked, but the risk of being caught was too great to read any further.

"Better get on with it," he told himself and opened the case. "Wow!"

A smooth, round stone the size of a football was sitting inside, glimmering with a radiant purple lustre. An intricate maze of grooves had been carved into its upper half. Zeke's scalp tingled as he examined the pattern. A strange desire to hold the stone boiled up inside him. It *wanted* his touch. He knew it, as if the thing were whispering to him.

He placed his finger at the beginning of the pattern, on the side of the globe. Slowly he traced along the complex path, upwards and inwards. The stone seemed to pull on his fingertip. He was sweating although the cabin wasn't hot. Then, at last, Zeke came to the very top.

The globe flickered like a candle going out.

With a crackle it collapsed into nothingness. Zeke, the Televator and the rest of the universe fell into this void. Voices echoed through darkness. Senseless voices that sounded like scraping rocks. A hideous inhuman face appeared out of nowhere and rushed towards him. Then came a lightening-white flare. Fire scorched his eyeballs and faded.

Zeke was standing in a rust-coloured desert. A black cloud hovered over distant mountains. What could it be? Smoke? Sand? His throat turned dry. The cloud was moving towards him.

Zeke wanted to run but his legs felt disconnected from the rest of his body. The thing in the air was travelling at a fantastic speed. Countless black particles were swirling inside. Insects?

Desperately Zeke glanced around for help. The desert was empty. The swarm was very near now and with a terrible swift movement, it swooped down and engulfed him.

Thousands of soft, furry bodies battered against him. Squirming, crawling, writhing, they quickly covered Zeke. He frantically tried to wipe them off, but there were too many. They weren't insects but symbols, *living symbols*!

Blinded, he fell into the sand. The shapes slithered up his legs, snaking through his hair. Zeke tried to scream but they flew into his mouth, forcing their way deeper. The creatures surged around his veins before, finally, flooding up into his brain.

He was lying on the floor of First Class. Thunder raged inside his skull. Had he fainted? The engines hummed in the background. The cabin was moving again.

Professor Magma was bending over Zeke, ranting furiously.

"How dare you interfere with the Orb of Words!"

Zeke struggled to speak over the throb of pain.

"*Crthrf gsh gaa nuk?*"

Magma pulled back.

"What did you say?"

Zeke rubbed his aching head.

"What is that thing?" he asked again.

Magma didn't reply.

Zeke took a deep breath and gathered his wits. First he glanced at the stone, sitting in its case as though nothing had happened. Then he stared into Magma's huge, burning eyes.

Oh no, he'd been caught red-handed!

"Are we okay in here?"

Both Zeke and Magma turned to the doorway. Stella Gates had poked her head into First Class.

Magma smiled at her through gritted teeth.

"Just peachy. Little Blue Boy here tripped and banged his head. I think he should lay down here for a while. I'll take care of him."

"You will not," said Zeke, suddenly afraid. Mustering his strength he stumbled to his feet. Their eyes met, Magma flashing his tiger glare again.

"And I'm fifteen, not a little boy."

Zeke staggered off to find his seat.

The gold ring spun up around the never-ending column, higher and higher. The landscape fell away. The horizon curved to the arc of the planet. The atmosphere chilled and thinned.

Inside Zeke slouched back in his chair.

"What happened?" Scuff demanded.

Zeke said nothing, nursing his tender head.

Scuff asked Pin-Mei, "So what did you see? In your premonition?"

Pin-mei's baby face clouded over.

"I'm not sure. Something dangerous."

Scuff gestured impatiently for her to continue.

"That thing in First Class made us stop and then made us start. I don't know how, I just feel it."

"Are you sure nothing happened while you were in there?" Scuff asked Zeke again.

"Nothing," he groaned.

What had really taken place? It seemed too crazy to confide to his new friends. And Martian runes? Zeke figured an archaeologist studied dead cultures. Did this mean non-human civilisation had once existed on Mars? If so it was the best kept secret in the Solar System. But why?

Pin-mei fiddled with her teddy bear.

"I've never had a premonition as clear as that before. Do you think it's because we're leaving the Earth's magnetic field?"

Scuff stroked his chin.

"Doubtful, sis, we weren't that high. And we're inside the magnetic field of the Televator."

Zeke looked up.

"Huh?"

"You didn't know? Any magnetic field disrupts psychic powers. That's why they only work at their best in Outer Space. Surely you'd heard that?" Scuff sounded surprised.

Pin-mei interrupted, "That's why the Chasm was built on Mars. It's geologically dead. No magnetic field."

Pin-mei and Scuff gave him a baffled look.

"Oh, I knew that," Zeke replied quickly, and cursed himself under his breath.

He turned his attention to the window and the tapestry of stars beyond. The sooner he got away from Magma the better. He checked his watch again and again, but the minutes crawled. The journey seemed never-ending.

Yet nothing lasts forever, not even the Televator. Although from the ground it appeared endless, it terminated eighty miles up. A crown-shaped satellite topped the tower, glittering with solar panels.

"Boys and girls, we'll shortly be arriving at the Hyperbola Spaceport," Stella bellowed into the microphone. "All change here for Luna Alpha, Luna Beta, Mars and the known universe. Do not undo your safety belts until the vehicle has come to a complete halt."

She forced a garlic-reeking smile at the passengers and dived into the galley.

A shadow engulfed the cabin. They had arrived.

Chapter Four

Hyperbola Spaceport

Zero gravity proved a clumsy business. At first the students found bouncing off the ceiling a giddy thrill. But weightlessness quickly became a drag, quite literally. Accidentally bumping into somebody was all too easy. Cries of 'ouch!' and 'watch out, moron!' rang out as they pulled themselves through the docking chamber.

They emerged into the huge steel gallery known as the Transit Deck. One by one they grabbed onto the guide cables, wondering what would happen next. A young African man with a cascade of dreadlocks and the white uniform of the Star Mariners floated gracefully towards them, as if by magic.

"Greetings newbies," he said in a slow lilting voice. "My name is Edward Dayo. It is my honour to perform today's translocation."

"I don't like being called a newbie," protested the pimply boy.

Dayo's broad smile sparkled in response. "I think it's preferable to the names you will be called at School. The older students will christen you Earthworms. If you are lucky."

"Whatever for, Mr Dayo?" Pin-mei asked, horrified at the very thought.

"Well you are from Earth. And you will live in the bowels of Mars. Perhaps like a worm?"

"I've been called worse," Scuff remarked sourly.

Pin-mei turned to Zeke. "We're hardly invertebrates, are we Zeke?"

Zeke didn't answer, his attention was fixed on Dayo. While the students had to push and pull themselves through the weightless environment he appeared to glide by willpower alone.

"Are you a Star Mariner?" he asked.

"Absolutely, young man. Third Class."

Zeke's heart leapt. He had never met a Mariner before. And here was one, a man who could leap across the galaxy in seconds. He could outrun a supernova or escape a black hole. Perhaps it was Zeke's imagination, but Dayo's eyes seemed to twinkle with stardust. Just as he imagined his father's did.

"Third class? Is that why you're on a cushy number?" the pimply boy asked.

"Cushy number?" Zeke repeated, surprised at such a cheeky attitude.

Dayo's enigmatic smile did not waver.

"The trip to Mars could be considered a trip around the block," he explained. "After all we Star Mariners are famous for piloting colony ships to the deepest parts of Outer Space."

Zeke frowned.

"Yes, about that, is it true they never come back?" the pimply boy asked.

The tiniest hint of uncertainty flickered on Dayo's face. He shifted in midair. "And whom do I have the honour of addressing?" he asked, beaming at the pimply boy.

"Snod. Jasper Snod," the boy said with an aloof pout.

"The Mars flight is my apprenticeship. My turn at the big wheel will come when I clock up enough flight hours. Now, everyone, if you will be so kind as to follow me, my Go-Ship awaits."

And then, quite effortlessly, Dayo pirouetted and glided away. A chorus of gasps escaped the new years.

"Psychokinesis," Scuff explained to an awestruck Zeke. "Happens to be my personal gift." His face contorted. With a quiver he started rising. Unlike the nimble Dayo he swayed like a buoy in rough waters.

"Psychokinesis. The power to move objects by thought?" Zeke asked.

"Very big objects," Pin-mei stated matter-of-factly as they watched Scuff's hefty backside drift past.

With a screech Scuff tipped upside down and rammed into Snod.

"Watch it, yak boy!" Snod barked.

Scuff blushed and grabbed onto a bulkhead, too embarrassed to speak.

For a quarter of a mile they hauled themselves along guide ropes. Edward Dayo bobbed ahead, encouraging them.

"Excellent. Much better than last year's intake."

"Why can't we move our bodies by mind power, like you?" Zeke called out from the back. His biceps were beginning to ache.

Dayo shrugged gently.

"Ah, that has taken me years of study, young newbie, years!"

Dayo's Go-Ship was docked at departure gate twelve. He opened the airlock and ushered them in.

"WAIT!"

It was Professor Magma, who was desperately trying to catch up. "I demand you take me to Mars. My tickets are all in order."

"No can do," Dayo said, politely but firmly. "This is a chartered flight, Professor, in the name of the school. There's a scheduled ship later. You can take that."

"Damn the Chasma School and its deviant brats. My work is of the highest importance. Top government clearance. Now let me in."

"No way, Professor. My ship is strictly for newbies."

Dayo stepped inside the airlock.

"Do you realise who you are talking too?"

"Totally!" the Mariner replied, and pushed a button. The airlock swished shut.

Magma pressed his nose to the window and caught sight of Zeke. The Professor shot him a carnivorous glare before reluctantly moving away.

"Why is he going to Mars?" Zeke enquired.

Dayo grinned. "There are times, little newbie, when it is safer to be the ostrich with its head in the sand. Now, please sit down and prepare yourself for Mars."

"I need a volunteer," Dayo said.

"Me, Sir, please me, me!" pleaded Snod.

"No, me!" Scuff begged.

A forest of hands shot up around the pyramid-shaped flight deck. Dayo was standing on the Mariner's Wheel in the centre while the students buckled their safety belts. His large unblinking gaze surveyed the scene.

"You, young Mariner." He pointed a long finger at Zeke.

The boy's heart sank. The last thing he needed was attention.

"Come and help me."

Zeke strode up to the Wheel, a podium full of computer consoles. A mass of wires dangled down around a man-sized scaffold covered with safety straps.

"Please fasten me in while I upload to the motherboard."

Dayo began tugging specific wires from the jumble and pressing them to his skull. The sensors were coated with nanocells that bonded painlessly to his skin. Zeke, meanwhile, strapped the Mariner onto the scaffold's foam cover.

Dayo spoke softly, so only the two of them could hear.

"Do you know why I chose you, my blue-headed friend?"

Zeke looked into those stardust-shimmering eyes. "Not really."

"There is something about you, something that separates you from to these other newbies."

Zeke reddened. Had Dayo caught him out? Some Mariners were telepathic. Could he read all the lies inside Zeke's brain?

"What was your score, in your ESP exam?"

"I- I don't remember."

"You don't remember? How peculiar. Yet there's something about you. What is your name, little Earthworm?"

"Zeke Hailey."

"For you, Zeke Hailey, Mars will be a revelation!"

Dayo had finished wiring himself into the ship's controls. He stretched out his arms and Zeke secured the Mariner's upper body.

"What's it like, Sir, translocation?"

"You will find out soon enough, young newbie."

"For you, I mean, doing it. Is it painful?"

"The Chasma School will teach you about such things and how to bear them. Now is not the time."

"Well then, how is it done?"

Dayo laughed. "How does an atom split? The atom doesn't know. But that doesn't stop it. You just calm your mind and think where you want to be. You will learn meditation techniques at the school, my inquisitive Earthworm."

Zeke finished the last strap.

"Please retake your seat," Dayo said. For the first time there was an edge of anxiety in his voice.

Zeke scurried back to his place.

Dayo surveyed the battery of dials. "All safety protocols checked and running to optimum proficiency," he announced to the ship's computer. Then he peered back at his passengers.

"Boys and girls, it's my honour to be translocating you today to the Red Planet. From here on in, may all your landings be lucky ones!" His wide smile lit up the compartment.

Edward Dayo relaxed back onto the scaffold. His eyes glazed over and his head drooped. Saliva trickled down his chin. His limbs convulsed. The deck lights faded and a humming noise filled the room. It grew louder and louder till Zeke feared his eardrums would burst—

—and the spaceship fell horribly silent. Cold, the dead empty cold of space, washed through Zeke's bones. In the pitch dark he felt his body twist and bend and stretch like rubber. Then there was no flight deck, no ship, nothing. Zeke was alone among stars.

Chapter 5

High Mars Orbit

The lights were back on. Zeke looked around the flight deck. Some of the group were sobbing, others were giggling hysterically. Pinmei groaned as she woke up from a faint. Edward Dayo, still wired to the motherboard, was laughing with a couple of the more robust students.

"Did you see stars?" Zeke asked Scuff who was sitting white-knuckled and rigid.

"They were stars? Thank God!"

"What?"

"I thought those were my brain cells exploding."

Zeke was itching for his first glimpse of Mars. Unfortunately it turned out to be a very unpleasant experience. Dayo freed himself and engaged a lever. The Mariner's Wheel glided up to the ceiling. This revealed a hidden chamber beneath the flightdeck.

"Into the sycamores. In pairs. You two first." Dayo pointed at Zeke and Scuff. A howl of protest pierced the air.

"Fatty and blue boy? Not fair," Jasper Snod protested with a jealous sneer.

Confused, Zeke shadowed Scuff up to the brink of the opening. Edward gestured to them to climb in and Zeke entered a tiny spherical compartment. A see-through bottom revealed the steel of the Go-Ship's hull. Padded bars pinned them to foam chairs.

"Earthworms, catch." Dayo grinned and threw them two tubs of triple strength sun block. "The Martian sunshine might be cool, but that solar radiation can still fry you. Oh, and you'll need these paper bags."

He closed the lid and was gone.

"You do know about this bit?" Scuff whispered, the colour draining from his face.

"No? What do you mean?"

A sudden jolt took their breath away. The sycamore slid along a few feet.

"Oh? This thing is suspended?" Zeke remarked. The vehicle reminded him of a cable car. Then came sounds of banging metal. Two more students were clambering into a second sycamore.

"Are we going on a tour?" Zeke asked innocently.

"W-We can't translocate onto the s-surface," Scuff stammered.

"Yes, I know that. Gravity's too powerful. We'd materialise in the wrong place."

"The one time they tried the ship arrived two miles below the surface. Instant death. Your molecules squashed in with rock molecules."

Another sharp movement yanked them further away from the flight deck. A third sycamore had slotted into place and a third couple were boarding.

"So does this take us to the Martian Televator?" Zeke continued.

"Bro! There *is* no Martian Televator. Budget cuts!"

"Then how will—"

The bubble lurched forward again. This time the see-through bottom slid over an opening in the hull.

"OH!" Zeke cried. They were dangling high above the cratered surface of Mars. He gripped the padded bars, as though at any second he might be sucked out into the deadly vacuum.

"We're about ninety miles up," Scuff squeaked.

With nothing but the Martian atmosphere between them and the far below landscape, Zeke's brain swam in its own juices. His stomach heaved viciously. Oh, that's what the bags were for! As the bag filled up with Zeke's breakfast he heard a sickening *ping*. The sycamore dropped.

"**S**omething's wrong," Zeke shouted. The sycamore was shaking like a roller coaster in an earthquake. Beneath them the mass of red splotches were growing bigger. The violent shuddering made speaking difficult.

"No…we're…fine," Scuff gasped through gritted teeth, eyes tightly shut.

"No…we're not," Zeke persisted. A tiny voice deep in his head was screaming. He looked at the digital dashboard in front of them. "We entered…atmosphere…three minutes ago."

"Yup…wings…release…soon."

The vehicle's design was based on the sycamore seed with two great spinning wings. These created air resistance, slowing the craft enough to launch the parachute. Any faster and the chute would rip.

As if in answer to Scuff's assurance an alarm buzzed. A message flashed on the dashboard. '*Malfunction: wings jammed.*'

"WE'RE DONE FOR!" Scuff shrieked.

Zeke glanced down. The splotches were forming into canyon walls, dust plains and volcanoes. The voice inside him yelled louder. THINK!!!

"Scuff…use your...psychokinesis…free the wings!"

"I…can't!"

"YOU MUST!"

Zeke reached out to his friend. The small gesture required superhuman effort. The increasing g-force was crushing them. Zeke squeezed Scuff's arm. The geek gulped and closed his eyes. But he couldn't concentrate, not now. Nothing happened.

"I CAN'T….SORRY…JUST CAN'T."

"COME ON…YOU CAN DO IT."

"CAN'T…YOU TRY."

The sycamore was growing hot. Unbearably hot. The craggy terrain was hurtling upwards.

"ZEKE, PLEASE…YOU DO IT"

"CAN'T!"

"YOU CAN!" Scuff implored him.

Zeke felt angry, terrified, sick and desperate. Without warning his feelings erupted.

"CAN'T…NOT…PSYCHIC!"

Bewilderment broke across Scuff's face.

"CHEATED…TO GET TO SCHOOL." Zeke spat the words out.

Scuff hissed an ugly name. Zeke cringed but he knew this was no time for excuses.

"YOU MUST…DO IT," he cried.

Scuff tried again. Zeke closed his eyes too. It might help, he thought frantically. Zeke pictured the wings on top of the Sycamore, jammed in their casings. He could see them, coiled up and waiting for their covers to blow. Zeke imagined a sycamore seed, wafting safely down from its tree. He focused hard on that image. With every fibre of his being he wished for the wings to unfurl.

A new message beeped, '*Wings operational*'.

"I did it!" Scuff yelped with elation.

Yet the voice inside Zeke's head said Scuff had nothing to do with it.

The sycamore's speed eased. With a sudden tug the parachute released into the pale Martian sky. Their descent slowed further. Underneath their feet the crimson canyons flowered into spurs and crests.

Scuff recovered his composure.

"Bro, you are done for!" he snarled. "The minute we get out of this tin can you'll be going back to Earth in chains."

Exhausted, reeking of vomit and ready to cry, Zeke landed on Mars.

Chapter Six

Mariners Valley

"**S**TOP!"

Zeke had his hand on the hatch wheel.

"Are you a moron as well as a liar?" Scuff bellowed.

The words stung.

"We've got to check we're in the right place," Scuff continued, poking at the sat-nav controls.

"The Valley is the biggest canyon in the Solar System, how could we miss?"

"I heard a sycamore went off course once and landed up on top. The idiot newbies opened the airlock. They were found clinging to the hull like a couple of Martian Popsicles."

Zeke shivered at the thought.

"Why don't the governments make Mars safe all over?"

"It's to do with the money."

Zeke gazed at him blankly.

"Don't they read in England? Haven't you heard about all the arguments at the UN, who's going to foot the bill etcetera. Terraforming is way behind schedule."

"But there's enough oxygen, right?"

"Sure, thanks to greenhouse gases and genetically modified bacteria. Oxygen levels are climbing. Two hundred years ago the air was so thin blood boiled in your veins. But Mars is far from Earthlike. Topside it's about as cosy as the summit of Mount Everest."

"So it's a good thing we're down in the Valley?"

Mariners Valley broke across the equator like a festering wound. As large as the U.S.A. it sank five miles below Martian sea level, not that there were any actual seas on Mars of course. At the bottom the air was thick enough for a comfortable existence. Zeke struggled to get his head around the science.

"So why doesn't the air leak out of the Valley, up into the lower pressure?"

Scuff threw him a withering glance. "Why doesn't Earth's atmosphere leak out into Space? Little thing called gravity." He finished examining the controls. "Wow, bang square in Ophir Chasma."

"What do all these names mean, anyway?"

"Chasma is Latin for canyon, bozo. Mariners Valley is made up of a whole bunch of them. Go on then, open up."

Zeke took a deep breath and opened the hatch.

Lower pressure sucked the stale air out with a whistle. A cold gritty dryness filled the sycamore. Mars lacked Earth's flora and humidity. Instead basalt and iron oxide dominated the environment. The Martian morning smelt like a cocktail of molten lead and dry ice.

Neither boy could wait to walk on Martian soil. With gravity one third of Earth's they both bounded effortlessly for the exit. But the opening wasn't wide enough for two and they jammed halfway out.

"Man, what a sight!" Scuff sighed in awe.

Zeke was dumbstruck, and for a moment forgot his 'new friend' was going to have him sent home.

The sun, rising in a tawny sky, lit up a jagged landscape. Canyon walls loomed high above them like an end-of-the-world tsunami. Across the valley spires of rock towered out from the gloom. Centuries of wind had gnawed them into strange precarious shapes. They resembled colossal petrified monsters, all claws, bones and teeth.

"It's so quiet!" Zeke whispered.

"You said it, bro! That's the absence of life and water."

"You could hear a pin drop twenty miles away!"

"I'm so damn lucky," Scuff said to himself. "I'm going to the best ever school and graduate an intergalactic hero! Sure beats a small town high school."

"Don't rub it in. We can't all be special," Zeke said, his lips in a grimace. Both boys clambered down from the sycamore.

A shadow fell across them. Another sycamore was idly descending. With a soft thud and cloud of ochre sand it landed nearby.

"Well, they can be the first to know," Zeke added bitterly.

Scuff looked at the ground, shifting uncomfortably from foot to foot. "Why did you do it, Zeke?"

"My dad's a Star Mariner. He left before I was born."

"That's what this is about? You miss your daddy?"

Zeke subdued an urge to punch his friend's froggy nose. That wouldn't solve anything!

"Bro! You can have mine gift-wrapped with ribbons. I can't believe you'd go through all this for your old man."

"Mum's told me so many stories about him. He was the funniest, bravest, kindest man she ever met. I just want to meet him."

"But how did you fool the examiners?"

"I sat next to a boy called Felix Dyer. He already knew he was psychic. He had absolutely no desire to go to Mars. We swapped answers without the teachers realising. Easy-peasy."

"And you thought you'd bluff your way through psych school?"

"Well, yes."

"Are you nuts?"

"Once I began it was kind of difficult to stop. I became a celebrity, interviews with the local webcasts, holomags, the whole circus. Mum started getting sponsorship deals. Without my father we've been pretty hard up. The money was great. I just went with the flow."

"Don't you think the teachers will notice?"

"Well, if you're so clever, psychic boy, tell me what we're not supposed to do?"

Scuff scratched his head for a moment, and then a light dawned on his face.

"We're not allowed to use our powers, not till we've passed the end of term exam."

Zeke nodded and added, "it would be too dangerous."

"But your dad isn't on the Big Pumpkin, is he? Why didn't you stow away on a colony ship?"

"Because we don't know where he went. His destination was top secret. But Mum thought people at the school might remember. Some of his classmates are now teachers. And all the Mariner records are all here."

"Gee, sounds like a plan."

"Right, a plan for disaster," Zeke replied, kicking a pebble.

Scuff threw him an odd expression.

"And you're sure you're not psychic?"

"I think I'd know. Don't you?"

"It's just—"

"Just what?"

A noise interrupted the conversation, like blades swishing through air. Although far away, in the crystal clear atmosphere it echoed around them.

"It's the school bus, picking us up," Scuff explained. He took a deep breath. "Sheesh! Two minutes on Mars and already life's complicated. Okay, Zeke, I'm on a whole new planet and you're my only bud. I really think you ought to 'fess up before you get into this any deeper, but they ain't going to hear it from me."

"You'll keep it secret?"

"Yes, your lordship," he replied in a ridiculous British accent.

Zeke's crooked grin broke across his face. But the grin faded as he realised Scuff was staring, wide-eyed, over his shoulder.

Scuff let out a scream.

"A giant bug, RUN!"

Zeek pivoted on one foot and saw something impossible. A huge metallic Millipede was crawling across distant boulders. Countless legs clicked up and down as it slivered over the landscape. Zeke's blood turned to ice.

He glanced back at Scuff who was doubled up with laughter.

"The expression on your face, bro! Priceless!"

He looked again. The segmented creature was actually a vehicle. Scuff made a tremendous effort to stop cackling.

"The school bus, bro. Hover cars don't work on a planet with no magnetism. Legs work better than wheels on this bumpy low-grav terrain. OUCH!"

A handful of gravel battered Scuff's chest. Zeke dusted his palms and waved at the Millipede.

"Over here! Before a certain boy genius drives me insane."

*T*he skies burned lava red. Firestones rained down upon a scene of hellish destruction. Zeke stood rooted, unable to move. It was coming. The great inhuman face was coming, a gargantuan face on many legs, crushing mountains underfoot. Terror as sharp as a knife twisted in Zeke's heart. The hideous face saw him. And it spoke! One word, ancient, alien and incomprehensible. But Zeke understood this word. 'Spiral'.

Zeke woke with a yell. He was at the back of the Millipede.

"Bad dream?" Pin-mei asked.

He sat up, confused and feverish. The Martian night had fallen and a land of shadows lay outside. Phobos, the tiny eye-shaped moon, shone feebly overhead. The constellations sparkled through unpolluted air like jewels. Zeke traced some of his favourites, Orion, Cassiopeia, and Pegasus. He marvelled how their patterns were unchanged. Even though he had travelled over fifty-five million miles their positions remained constant. The vastness of the universe was beyond imagination. For an instant he felt dizzy, as if he might fall off this tiny planet into the endless pit of space.

"Bro, the stars here are just the same as back in Britsville."

It was Scuff, munching on a bar of Martian chocolate. Zeke gave him a ferocious stare. Was the geek reading his thoughts again?

The Millipede, piloted by two school Mariners, had spent a long, tiring day trawling the lowlands. One by one the sycamores were located and their occupants rescued. Some had landed in better condition than others. Snod had sustained a black eye and was in a foul mood. One girl was found wandering aimlessly and singing to herself. Pin-mei, on the other hand, was gleefully munching her mother's homemade rice-cakes.

"That's fun. Can we do it again?" she giggled.

Each student was welcomed heartily by the teachers and treated to steaming soup and heaps of Martian chocolate. Despite the bitter taste Scuff gobbled down fifteen cherry-coloured bars before Zeke nodded off.

"We're there!" Pin-mei squeaked.

She pointed through the windscreen. For the first time in his life Zeke beheld the Chasm.

A thousand lit windows flickered against the lifeless alien night. They illuminated a fortress of gloomy towers. Originally tunnelled out of natural catacombs, the School had expanded over time. New wings had crept outwards and upwards; parapets, turrets and arches. The structure brooded against the cliff like a giant coral.

"Gosh!" was all he could say, mouth agape.

The Millipede was nearing the great stone entrance. Three words were engraved into the slab, *thought, magnetism, gravity.*

"Of these three thought is the most powerful," the students all chanted, even Scuff and Pin. Twenty pairs of eyes lit up with psychic energy, glowing like diamonds in the dark. A rush of coldness tugged at Zeke's lungs. He was alone, on another planet, and among freaks.

Chapter Seven

The Ophir Chasma School for Psychic Endeavour

With a hiss the Millipede slowed to a standstill. The students wearily staggered out into a school courtyard. Clumsy, mud-coloured buildings rose up on all sides. Zeke imagined a city of monstrous termite mounds and shivered. Whether from shock or the bitter Martian night he couldn't tell.

"You're looking seriously freaked out," Scuff said in a shaky voice.

"I am. Stop reading my mind."

"I told you already, bro. I'm no telepathist."

Zeke shrugged and glanced around at his peers. They were looking red-eyed and emotional, as the reality of an alien planet sunk in. They might never see their families again. A tall, olive-skinned girl was crying softly, with a crumpled letter in her hand. Even the revolting Jasper Snod was silent, his eyes fixed on his feet. Zeke thought of his own mother far across the gulf of space. What was she doing now, he wondered? An image of their tearful farewell at the airport flashed into his mind. It was too painful. Instead he focused on his father, up there somewhere, lost among the stars. He had to find him! He would find him!

Footsteps chipped on the stony ground. A brown uniformed figure flanked by two assistants was approaching.

"Stand lively and listen up," barked the stranger. "I'm in charge of Supplies and Requisitions."

"He means he's the caretaker," Snod whispered to a neighbour.

The man glared at Snod as if he belonged under a microscope. "Did you say something young Earthworm?"

"N-no," Snod replied, avoiding eye contact.

"I am Quartermaster Stubbs, here to welcome you and sort out sleeping arrangements. No doubt you're all exhausted after a day spanning two solar time zones, but bear with me and we'll get this fixed a.s.a.p."

Stubbs was a stout man with the face of a rhinoceros and a military haircut. He browsed a long scroll of names. As they waited Pin-mei slipped her hand into Zeke's, and let out a massive yawn.

"I'm space-lagged. We've gone two whole days without a proper sleep."

"Any minute now and we'll be in Snoresville," Scuff remarked.

She squeezed Zeke's hand. "Zeke, I was so scared back on the Televator."

"We all felt the same."

"But you made me feel safe. I think you're good at it."

"What?"

"Keeping people safe. Promise you'll look after me. Be my Martian big brother."

Zeke looked down at her, at the dark circles round her eyes and the grubby cheeks. She seemed so small and vulnerable. A sense of foreboding trembled in his chest.

"Of course! Promise."

Scuff poked a finger in his mouth.

"Pass the vomit-bag, bro."

"Listen up," the Quartermaster began. "I'll read out everyone whose parents prepaid. Your rooms are in East Wing, and very nice suites they are too. Superb views and operational toilets. Now is there anyone who hasn't prepaid?"

There was a long pause before Zeke raised his arm.

"Aha, one of those families," Stubbs remarked with a scornful expression. "It's not often we get students from the bottom of society."

Most of the students hooted loudly, glad for a distraction from their homesickness. Zeke buried his head in his palms as his cheeks burned. Why did he come from a poor single-parent family? Why couldn't he have a high-flying father? It wasn't fair. A wave of despair washed through him. Planet Earth, Mum and his old life suddenly seemed so remote, as though they belonged to a prehistoric era that was gone forever.

Pin-mei stood on the tips of her soles and whispered in his ear. "I learnt an English word for these kids." Giggling, she said it.

Zeke turned paler than the light of the Martian moons.

"Now, now, if I'm to be your honorary big brother I can't have that kind of language," he said, hiding his embarrassment.

Scuff glanced over at Zeke. "Hey, having a rich daddy isn't everything. You should've seen the smile on my old man's face when I left for Tibet."

Before Zeke could say anything Scuff moved away.

Stubbs looked up from his long list. "Is your name Hailey?"

"Yes, Sir."

"OK, we have a room for you on the lower levels. Part of the original caverns. No windows and lousy ventilation, but beggars can't be choosers, can they?"

"No, Sir."

Stubbs gestured to the crowd.

"When I say your name go to my assistants who'll sort out your first year uniforms. Silver-coloured tunic and breeches with stiff space-boots. Compulsory for all newbies. And don't forget the extra forty minutes in bed."

The sea of faces stared blankly.

"You're on Mars, people! The day here is thirty-nine minutes longer than Earth. At midnight the clocks all stop and thirty-nine minutes later start up again."

"I knew that," Scuff insisted.

The Quartermaster held up his scroll.

"Almera? Juanita Almera?"

The olive-skinned girl wiped her eyes and stumbled forward.

"**M**um?"

Zeke opened his eyes. Instead of the familiar chaos of his bedroom he saw the cold walls of a cave. His new room was a pothole carved by an underground river billions of years ago. As for Mum, she was over fifty-five million miles away, on another world, under another sky. A nausea tingled the pit of his stomach. With a deep breath he ignored it.

He glanced around the cave-room, as bare as a prison cell. The only touch of colour was the framed photo of his father he'd placed on the bedside cabinet. He stared at the bronzed, handsome face with its lopsided smile.

"Morning, Dad. We're a step closer. An enormous step. I'm on Mars now, at the Chasm. Where you grew up."

He was talking to a photograph. Zeke suddenly felt foolish and returned his attention to his living quarters. Later he could decorate the place with his posters of the famous astronomy museum, the London Galactarium. With a sad smile he recalled all the Saturday afternoons he'd spent there. The main attraction was the Star Dome, with its old-fashioned depiction of the night sky. Hundreds of lights in the ceiling lit up in changing patterns to illustrate the constellations. Over time Zeke had memorised them all.

Then Zeke noticed the mountain bike, propped against the wall, plugged in and charging. A golden label dangling from the frame read simply, 'a gift from the United Nations.' Presumably every new student got one. The logo down the sidebar proclaimed it to be a *Rover*, manufactured specifically for Mars.

It had thicker tyres than Zeke's bike back on Earth, adapted for the harsh terrain. The gears were all automatic. A small, computerized console sat on the handlebars, equipped with sat-nav, wireless and radar.

An idea flashed through Zeke's mind. He fished out a DVD in a crinkled envelope from his rucksack.

"This'll come in handy," his mother had said when she packed it.

The handwritten note on the back read:

Use this software to upgrade any kind of vehicle. It's called ALBIE and has a hundred and one useful apps. C.H.

The sight of his father's scrawl filled him with emptiness. Pushing that feeling aside Zeke inserted the disc. The bike's console flickered for a few moments.

"Please identify owner," the bike said, its voice as metallic as a wind chime.

"Zeke Hailey."

"Voice recognition software locked to Master Zeke Hailey."

It would only work for him!

"Upgrades complete. Albie fully installed. Any further requests, Master Zeke?"

Zeke scratched his blue hair, filthy with the grime of two planets.

"Um, well, what time is it?"

"Eight forty-six am, Martian Mean Time, Sir."

"WHAT!!"

He was late for his first day! Zeke leapt in the icy shower, threw on his stiff, itchy new uniform and dashed out.

The Chasma School was a gloomy labyrinth of corridors, cloisters and classrooms. Zeke felt he was scurrying through the tunnels of an ant nest.

After several wrong turns he found a great steel door proclaiming 'Congregation Hall.' A digital notice board flashed the class schedules: Psychokinesis, Translocation, Telepathy, Precognition, Psychometry, Chakra Awareness, Remote Viewing, and Astral Phasing. A shiver tickled his spine.

"Talk about weird science!" he muttered, as he pushed his way in.

On his right sat rows and rows of students. The newbies were at the front, with miserable homesick expressions. The teachers were all seated to the left on a stage. The entire Hall listened intently to an African woman on a podium. She wore the ceremonial white robes permitted to only one person in the galaxy—the Chasm's School Principal!

Zeke recognised her at once. Henrietta Lutz was famous from Mercury to Pluto, famous for a heart of steel and a will of iron. Her pursuit of excellence was ferocious and her discipline ruthless. Even the leaders of Earth called her Ma'am.

The woman froze in mid-sentence and scowled ferociously at Zeke. Who dared interrupt the Principal of the most important school in history? Zeke blushed redder than the surface of Mars.

At length she spoke. "You, with the blue hair, how good of you to join us."

"*Dthothruthruuk mrnstx.*" Zeke's jaw dropped. He couldn't even speak!

"Are you mad, boy?"

Zeke said nothing, desperately searching for a spare chair.

"And your name is?"

"Zeke Hailey, Miss," he said, inching towards the aisle.

"That is 'Ma'am' to you, boy."

"Y-Yes Miss, I mean M-Ma'am," he stammered.

"I hope this shocking lack of punctuality will not be a regular occurrence."

"No, Ma'am. Can I sit down, Ma'am?"

"Can you? How would I know the limit of your physical abilities? Do you suffer from a sore backside? Haemorrhoids?"

A few dozen throats erupted in malicious laughter.

"N-no, Ma'am."

"Then surely you can. The question is MAY you?"

"May I sit down, Ma'am?"

"You may. And submit an essay to the school secretary before five p.m. entitled: The Merits Of Punctuality."

The Hall rang with more laughter. Zeke sloped off to the back row, crushed. Principal Lutz returned to her speech.

"Where was I? Oh yes. I'd like to offer the new students a warm greeting. I'd like to but I can't. Mars is too dangerous."

The more sensitive newbies gasped.

"So you expected a planet of milk and cookies? It's my duty to dash those hopes. Mars is a death trap. Stray out of Mariners Valley and you'll freeze solid. But don't think you're safe down here. Perils lurk around every boulder. Flash floods, rock falls, and oh, the quicksand! I lose so many children to the quicksand.

Just as deadly are our fellow humans. The mining camps, the oxygen factories, the colonies, about as law-abiding as the Wild West. You're all banned from these settlements for good reason."

Principal Lutz paused to draw breath. Zeke glanced around at the spellbound audience. This woman was obviously an old hand at putting the fear of God into newbies.

"And now a story. Yes honoured students, a tale of the end of worlds, of heroism, and most of all, a twist. Every one of you is a character in this frightful story. So listen carefully, it just might save your life."

Chapter Eight

The Congregation Hall

Principal Lutz paused and nodded sternly. The teachers and older students filed out of the cavernous room. A tall girl with a huge blond ponytail paused at Zeke's row. Her face was so caked in make-up she looked like a doll. She let out a mock yawn.

"Same old routine, year in, year out."

She popped a sweet in her cherry-coloured lips.

"So you're the new Earthworms? Even more feeble-looking than last year's."

Her gaze fell on Snod.

"You, zit face. I might have a vacancy for you, see me at break."

She strode off, her ponytail swishing from side to side.

Lutz was alone with the newbies. She clicked her fingers and the photon lamps dimmed. Slowly, with arms spread-out, she levitated from the floor. Bobbing gently, she gestured to the students.

"Oh!" Zeke gasped as he rose from his seat. Along with the rest of his peers he floated upwards.

"Takes powerful psychokinesis to pull off a stunt like this!" Scuff puffed. He tried to steady himself but overbalanced and swung upside down.

Bubbles of glowing gas ignited throughout the Hall.

"It's the Milky Way!" Zeke cried. He knew his astronomy.

Countless stars were burning against the backdrop of the universe. He reached out and touched a diamond-bright nova, but there was nothing.

"Hologram projectors. In the ceiling," Pin-mei explained, poking her face through a cloudy nebula.

Lutz cleared her throat.

"Long ago lived a goddess."

The students cooed as a beautiful woman twirled and skipped her way across the galaxy. She curled up inside her blue and green cloak, transforming into the Earth.

"She had as many names as there are languages. I call her Gaia. Gaia dancing for aeons around her father, Sol."

A fireball emerged from the glittering tapestry and took Gaia into its orbit.

"But Gaia was alone. Her seas were empty, her mountains silent. So she became a mother, our first mother, a virgin mother. Her child was Life."

The stars changed into single-celled protozoa and amoebas.

"Her child was one and many. And Gaia was a wise mother, always improving her children, making them better. Over time she added lungs, limbs and brains."

The creatures morphed into jellyfish, fish, frogs, lizards, monkeys and, finally, unborn human babies.

"Gaia's last child was her best. His name was Man and he was very clever, indeed, a little too clever."

One infant matured speedily, reaching adulthood in moments. Around him trees sprang up, thickened, then solidified into skyscrapers. A city hummed with cars, jets and rockets.

"Sometimes cleverness is another word for stupidity. Man was cunning and greedy, but tragically shortsighted. Perhaps a devil whispered in his ear. Too proud to remain a child, Man yearned to become a god. Man could not create life like his mother, but he could invent. Yet his machines were flawed. Amid all this busyness and invention Man made a terrible mistake. He poisoned his own mother."

The scene melted into the Solar System. The spinning Earth unfolded back into the woman, now old and diseased. Pin-mei choked back a sob.

"It took Man a couple of centuries to realise what he'd done, by then too late. Yes, he filled ozone holes and cooled global warming. But even his magic couldn't fix this deeper problem. Gaia was slowly dying, beyond cure. So Man, with his endless ingenuity, cast around for a new mother."

Mars rotated into view.

"This mother was barren and ancient. But Man didn't let little things like that stand in his way. He had many tricks to rejuvenate Mars. Man warmed her icy desert. He pumped her full of gas. He scattered germs and sowed seeds. And so, just as a world made Man, Man made a world."

A quick succession of images merged one into another. Mirrors in high orbit reflecting the sunlight. Comets rerouted from deep space melting in the upper atmosphere. Massive cargo ships ferrying hydrogen from Jupiter. Oxygen-converting bacteria drifting on the air. Genetically modified grass sprouting from the ochre soil.

"Man proposed The Five Century Plan—abandon Earth but save Mars. But The Plan proved costly. Taxpayers revolted, governments toppled. Meanwhile Man made fresh discoveries. Finally he understood the three sacred powers of existence: gravity, magnetism and thought. And of these three forces, thought is the most powerful."

The lightshow whizzed out of the rapidly growing Martian pastures and focused on a small boy surrounded by craggy peaks.

"Thoughts can speak to each other without sound. They can move objects, predict the future or see through walls. Their greatest ability is to change locations, *in the twinkling of an eye!*"

Electricity sparked deep in the boy's eyes. The rocky landscape blurred. The boy found himself inside a classroom, looking at a map of constellations.

"This skill is called translocation. Moving between places, however far apart, by thought not action. You see, reality is nothing more than our perception of atomic structure. Once you understand this, you can sidestep the physical dimension and be wherever you wish to be."

The sky-map zoomed out and filled the Congregation Hall with stars again. Gigantic spacecrafts cruised into sight, Far-Ships built for long-distance galactic travel.

"Man dropped the Five Century Plan in favour of a plan B. Cosmic Migration! All that was required were psychics, the one-in-a million gifted enough to power spaceships. And so Man channelled his energies into nurturing psychics. The Space Mariners Institute was founded to recruit, train and employ these gifted youngsters."

One by one the Far-Ships shimmered and vanished. The stars expanded and fused to form Lutz's face, enlarged and radiant.

"This is why Mankind needs you, tomorrow's Mariners. Every day cosmologists detect more earthlike habitable planets. New Gaias are calling to us from across the heavens. We're the ones who get there. We are the saviours of humanity."

She stopped to take a deep breath.

"Now, I hope you were taking notes because this is in the half-term quiz. Any questions?"

The immense face, both forbidding and benign, smiled at her audience.

"Yes," a lone voice piped in the dark.

Surprise burst across her enormous visage.

"Someone actually wants to ask something? The first time in twenty years! Who is it? You again?"

Zeke squirmed beneath her gaze but he was determined to speak.

"Why does nobody ever come back from the colonies?"

The glowing countenance frowned.

"You'll find out for yourself one day. Don't worry your young head about details. As saviours of the human race we need to focus on the big picture. So if there are no more—"

"Principal Lutz, one more question please."

Her mammoth eyebrows arched in amusement, waiting for him to go on.

"Have there ever been Martians?"

A chorus of titters rippled around the Hall. But the image of the Principal sighed.

"Ah yes. There were."

"Why is it secret?"

"It's not secret. It's classified. For our own safety."

The hologram face reddened and craters appeared across its huge cheeks. Mars reappeared, spinning.

"Life did flourish here, during the Hesperian Era. That was nearly two billion years ago. An entire ecosystem that vanished along with all its oxygen. Our best archaeologists have scoured Mars for decades but few clues remain. No record of their appearance, their culture or history survives. Only the extremely rare artefact that occasionally turns up in the sand."

The revolving planet changed. The surface smoothed over. Grooves multiplied around its circumference, forming patterns and symbols. Zeke's heart skipped a beat. It was Professor Magma's orb!

"Only four have been found and each proved deadly. If you ever, EVER, come across a Hesperian relic, whatever you do, do NOT touch it. Do I make myself clear?"

The shocked students murmured in agreement. The orb picture dissolved to reveal the woman herself, standing at her podium. They were all seated again, as if nothing had happened.

Chapter Nine

Ophir Chasma

Zeke pushed the pedals faster and faster. The Rover raced effortlessly along the dirt track. After a lifetime in Earth's gravity, cycling on Mars was easy.

He twiddled the brake lever, which activated the rear cam. A holoscreen popped up above the handlebars. He searched for a glimpse of the others. Nothing but dust. Then Zeke lifted his head. The cool Martian sun was dipping to the west. Ahead a vast slope towered five miles high, the remains of a colossal prehistoric landslide.

"I LOVE MARS!" he hollered at the empty canyons.

An outcrop of tall, sharp rocks like switchblades loomed in front. Zeke pedalled between them. As he emerged from their shadows the path dropped sharply. The bike plummeted but Zeke skilfully skidded to a halt. Moments later, Pin-mei zoomed over the rim. She lost her balance and landed in a cloud of red sand.

"Mars is fun!" she smirked. But the smirk was short-lived. Pin-mei picked a handful of dirt and allowed it to drop through her fingers. "But I still miss my mummy and daddy."

Zeke pulled her up, trying to think of something a big brother might say. A few kind words to chase away her glum expression. As nothing popped into his head he decided to change the subject.

"Where's Scuff?"

"Here," came a voice.

They glanced up to see the Canadian, dismounted and pouting.

"Pedal-power is for jocks, not boy geniuses," he grumbled, and gingerly walked his bicycle down to join them.

"I brought chrysanthemum milk and rice cakes," Pin-mei said more cheerfully.

The friends sat down on a convenient boulder. A single furrow formed on Pin-mei's smooth forehead. A milk carton rose from her backpack as if on a string. It glided through the air and landed on Zeke's lap. A second floated into Scuff's grasp and a third to Pin-mei. Three sweet dumplings, coloured candy pink, also levitated up and out. Scuff hungrily swallowed one.

"Pin's getting good at psychokinesis," Zeke said.

"It's easier on Mars," Pin-mei replied.

"The weaker gravity?"

"Yes, and no magnetic field. I feel like my mind's waking up."

"Me too!" Scuff interrupted, clearly a little jealous.

He stared intensely at his yellow carton. It wobbled into the air and then—KERSPLAT—exploded! Zeke and Pin-mei tried very hard not to laugh. Scuff was dripping with milk.

"You need to practice," Zeke said through gritted teeth.

"At least I'm not a bad luck magnet, bro."

"Huh? You mean me upsetting the Principal?"

"And, like, stopping the Televator, jamming the wings on my sycamore, not to mention your hallucinations."

After seeing the orb in Lutz's 'slideshow' Zeke had blurted out what really happened onboard the Televator. It all seemed too unbelievable, not to mention scary, to keep secret. The truth had escaped him like air from a balloon. At first his friends had reacted with scepticism, then bewilderment and finally concern.

"It wasn't a hallucination. It was more of…a message," Zeke replied.

"You should tell the Principal. Remember what she said. Martian relics can be fatal," Scuff warned. Pin-mei nodded in agreement.

"That would only show I went through Magma's belongings without permission. And I'm not sure I trust Principal Lutz. She's strange. But Magma is up to something and I'm going to find out what, before I speak to the authorities."

"Don't you think you'll be too busy fooling the instructors?" Pin-mei asked with a sweet smile. Every muscle in Zeke's body tightened. *She knew!* He threw an accusing glare at Scuff.

"Bro! I had to tell someone. And she is your bud."

The Chinese girl placed her hand on Zeke's and fixed him with her intense stare. Sometimes, Zeke thought to himself, Pin-mei seemed a lot older than eleven.

"Scuff and I have a plan," she said.

"I'm open to suggestions."

"Just stick close to us in class. If the teachers tell you to perform a psychic act we can do it for you. I like being part of a secret."

Zeke grinned. "Well I don't think that will be necessary. By the start of next term and psychic practice I'll be long gone."

Pin-mei's face dropped.

"But you can help me track down my dad's records," Zeke added quickly.

"How will you do that, smart stuff?" Scuff asked in a sceptical voice.

"Um, well, I'm still working on that one. But they must keep records somewhere."

"Then all you have to do is get back into space and hitch a ride on a Far-Ship going in the right direction. While you're at it, why don't you lasso a black hole and ride it side-saddle?"

"Hey, I've got this far, haven't I?" Zeke snapped, trying to sound confident.

Pin-mei beamed at him. "Zeke is very clever for a non-psychic. If he says he can do it, he can. Don't forget, thought is the most powerful force in the universe."

"Hey look!" Scuff pointed to the distance.

A column of dirt, caught by a breeze, danced across the plain.

"A mini-whirlwind!" Pin-mei cooed.

"Albie, do you register that weather phenomena? What is it?" Zeke asked.

His bike bleeped into life. "It's called a dust devil, Mr Zeke. Hot air rising off the ground through cold air starts to rotate, commonly found in desert environments. Some Earth cultures think of them as bad spirits. The Martian dust-devils have been observed since the first landings."

The dust devil petered out and another picked up a few feet further on. Pin-mei stared strangely at the tiny cyclone.

"Pin?" Zeke asked.

She shook herself. "There's something really creepy about them. As though—"

Scuff stamped his foot. "Enough with the cloud spotting. My belly's busting and it's dinnertime."

"OK, last one back to School's a Martian tomato," Zeke cried, and pedalled off.

The Cranny Cafeteria had been a simple crack in the cliff for millions of years. Then the school's architects came along and transformed it into a glassed-off canteen. The sweeping view of Mariners Valley was breathtaking.

Zeke and his friends walked in to find a long, hungry queue of students. At the front automacs were serving food over a counter. These robotic workers resembled bulky vending machines with extendable arms and legs.

"Cajun chicken with fries," Scuff ordered.

"With ketchup, Sir?" the machine droned.

"Sure, you got low cal?"

"Yes, Sir, anything else?"

"Nope."

The automac made a mechanical grunt and the meal popped out of an opening in its belly. The spicy smell tugged at Zeke's stomach.

"Same for me."

Once Pin-mei had her noodle soup they found a spare table. All three dived ravenously into their meals.

"Oi! Move!"

It was Snod, flanked by a couple of beefy older boys.

"This is Trixie's table. Don't you know anything?"

"Sorry, we were here first. Can't we just share?" Zeke suggested.

Snod flashed them a look of alarm. "Trixie Cutter rules the roost here. She's a powerful psychokinetic. Stronger than some of the teachers."

"Sheesh, I'm wetting myself," Scuff replied casually.

The tall girl with the perfect ponytail strode up, carrying a tray of salad. She smiled at them with all the charm of a piranha.

"I'm counting to three then you Earthworms better disappear," she said.

Zeke felt his temper rising.

"We aren't going anywhere."

Electricity crackled deep in the girl's eyes. Zeke's dinner plate flipped a somersault and chicken sauce splattered his head. Scuff suffered a worse indignity. An invisible hand pulled back the waistband of his slacks and dumped the contents of his plate inside. Pin-mei's chair toppled and she fell to the floor. Her bowl whizzed into the air, drenching the three friends in soup.

Zeke leapt to his feet. Before he could protest a chicken wing rammed itself into his mouth. He began choking.

"You really must chew first. Let me help," Trixie said in a cold voice, and chucked her glass of water over his head.

Spluttering, he coughed out the wing and rubbed his eyes.

"Still here, bluey?" Trixie sneered. "Your pals had more sense."

Zeke turned to see Scuff and Pin-mei bounding for the door. There was nothing he could do but join the retreat.

That night Zeke's sleep was plagued by nightmares. He dreamt again of the fiery landscape. This time, instead of the giant inhuman face, it was Trixie Cutter as big as a skyscraper. She came storming over the smoking volcanoes. Laser beams zapped from her eyeballs and incinerated everything they touched.

Zeke turned to flee and saw a tall brawny Mariner beckoning in the distance. His father! Before Zeke could move a huge wall burst from the red soil, blocking his escape and cutting off his father.

One large word was carved into the bricks.

$$\bigcirc(\dashv\ulcorner\lrcorner\div\!\!\!/ \dashv\ulcorner\Omega$$

Zeke read the letters aloud, struggling with syllables impossible for human vocal chords.

"*Khriinthnga.*"

Inexplicably Zeke recognised the word. The Spiral-Killer!

Chapter Ten

Translocation for beginners

Zeke glanced at his schedule. He was definitely in the right place. A long flight of steps had led him down to a subterranean chamber and the creaky door before him. Not the impressive location he'd expected for the most important subject in the solar system. Telepathy classes took place in the shiny new annexe across the courtyard and at least Psychokinesis 101 was above ground. The name over the doorway proclaimed a Mariner Adrian Knimble. Zeke wondered what kind of teacher passed his working hours at the bottom of this hole.

Inside the windowless classroom the purple and silver of photon-lamps danced on the shadows. Zeke took a seat in the back row and looked around. Replicas of famous rockets dangled from the ceiling: a Saturn V, a Russian Tsyclon, the early Go-Ships. The walls were decorated with atomic symbols and equations, quite meaningless to Zeke.

"It's not as difficult as you think."

Zeke jumped to his feet. He hadn't realised anyone else was there.

A bald, wiry man with a goatee beard stood by the plasma-board.

"Excuse me, Sir! I didn't see you."

"You couldn't have," replied the teacher with an Australian accent.

The penny dropped. Mariner Knimble had translocated into the classroom. Well, it was his field.

"An early student. This indicates a keen thirst for knowledge or—"

Zeke puffed out his chest and tried to look scholarly.

"—a total lack of friends, and therefore nothing better to do."

Zeke deflated rapidly. The teacher was right.

"Name?"

"Hailey."

"Hailey you say? And with hair the colour of ink!"

Knimble breezed down the aisle. His deep, pale eyes gazed through Zeke like an X-ray. "Any relation to Cole Hailey?"

At last someone who remembered!

"My father, Sir. Did you know him?"

"Never play poker with a telepath. Your father won a fortune in Martian dollars from me."

Zeke forced a smile.

"So he was good at mind-reading then?"

"Skilled all-rounder, as I recall. Ah, I see! You were too young to get acquainted before he went Deep Side. Sad."

Knimble's faraway stare pierced Zeke briefly then focused beyond, as though observing the far side of the galaxy.

"What did you think of Dad's mission?" Zeke said, trying to sound casual.

"His mission? Where did he go?"

"You don't know?"

"Why should I?—Oh, you don't know either? You're fishing, but why?"

Zeke squirmed under the Mariner's scrutiny. He decided to change the subject.

"My hair? Mum likes to say a cartridge of—"

"Nano-dye fell on your head. I see you have inherited your father's jokes, as well as his peculiar hair," Knimble remarked dryly.

Thankfully, at that moment, a couple of Zeke's classmates dived through the door.

"Ah, come in Earthworms, come in." Knimble beamed and held out his arms in welcome.

More students piled in quickly. Knimble greeted them all, ticking names off the digital register, before returning to the front.

"Firstly, congratulations on entering the Ophir Chasma School for Psychic Endeavour. Or the Chasm as you probably call it."

The class giggled politely.

"Of all the psychic sciences Translocation is the most crucial. As Principal Lutz explained in her welcoming speech, it makes the Cosmic Migration happen. Conventional space travel takes thousands of years just to get from one star to another. Turtle travel I call it.

"But thanks to us, humanity is sprinting across the Milky Way like hares. This is Man's defining moment, all thanks to translocation. Psychokinesis, precognition, telepathy, well, they're just party tricks in comparison.

"So, can anyone explain the science?"

The Mariner surveyed the class for an answer. Only one student was cocky enough to reply. Scuff raised a chubby finger in the air.

"The Big Bang Theory, String Theory and various other theories all agree that the Universe started out the size of a dime—"

"Canadian propaganda! I heard it was a penny!" Snod cried.

"Quiet!" Knimble said through a steely smile.

Scuff sent a look of scorn in Snod's direction and went on. "On the sub-subatomic level the Universe is still that size. But our brains see the world in three dimensions—"

"In other words the dimensions of length, width, depth. What mathematicians call Euclidean Geometry."

"Yes, Mariner Knimble. The average human can't see the interconnectedness of everything. In fact he'd go totally nuts if he did. Then a famous egghead, Doctor Kajacofski, came up with the Theory of Unrelativity. This suggested the psychic brain could sidestep reality, pass through the sub-subatomic level, and emerge anywhere in the Universe."

Scuff paused to take breath. A sea of baffled faces surrounded him.

"And your name is?" Knimble asked.

"Surly Bum-Brain," Snod piped up, but the entire class ignored him.

"Barnum, Sir."

"Very good, young Barnum. Very good indeed. I'll take it from there. Let me demonstrate."

Mariner Knimble drew himself to his full height. He took a step towards the front desks. On the second step his eyes crackled. On the third he blurred and by the fourth he was gone. Mouths dropped all around the classroom.

"Over here!"

Twenty heads swivelled a hundred and eighty degrees. Knimble sat on an empty desk munching an apple.

"Pinched this from the canteen. Don't tell the automacs."

More giggles.

"So I just bypassed laws of physics. I walked from here to the canteen and back by the most direct route, the sub-subatomic. But why couldn't I pick this apple from a tree on Earth?"

Scuff yawned and raised his hand once again.

"Someone else?"

Pin-mei gave a little wave. "Gravitational distortion. To get to Earth you must escape Mars' gravity. But just as we can't jump off Mars, we can't translocate off it either."

"And trying to do so would be very, very dangerous. That's why interplanetary travel starts and ends up there." Knimble pointed heavenwards.

All this science was hurting Zeke's brain. He raised a hand.

"So psychics can just imagine their way across the galaxy?"

"In time, with years of practise and some technological assistance, yes."

"And other galaxies, could we think ourselves there?"

"In theory, yes. But no human has the brain power to get that far, even with our bio-mechanical boosters."

Scuff waved his hand. "String Theory states that countless parallel universes exist. Have the Mariners ever tried to translocate between dimensions?"

Knimble laughed as if Scuff had said something very stupid. "Do parallel universes exist? Probably. Can we visit them? Never."

The students stared at him vacantly.

"Strewth! Okay, imagine the universe is a motorway. Every time a new universe is created it's like the motorway branching off into two. Then four and so on till there are gazillions of motorways running parallel. You are a car driving along one motorway. There's no way of leaving your motorway and joining another as once they split they are separate forever."

"So why not go backwards till you come to an exit?" Scuff asked.

"In case you hadn't noticed motorways are one-way. The same with universes. You'd have to travel back in time, which is also impossible. But even if you could, and tried to change lanes you would end up on the same motorway. That's what we call Quantum Decoherence. The motorway would adjust itself at a faster-than-light speed. You'd never even notice."

Knimble paused and scanned his classroom. Realising he had confused everyone, he coughed and changed tack.

"Now I want to teach you a most invaluable lesson."

The teacher skipped back to his desk, picked up a photograph and circulated it among the desks. The first student to see it turned a very nasty shade of green. Snod pointed at her and guffawed. Then the photo appeared under his nose. He bolted from the room, hand on mouth.

Zeke braced himself as his turn approached. Knimble flashed the picture before him. It showed a man leaning against a wall. Zeke could only see the man's left half. He peered closer.

"Oh…!"

The unfortunate man's right side had completely merged with the wall. Half a mouth gaped in a frozen scream. The veins in his face had all popped, colouring his skin avocado purple. Not surprisingly, he was quite dead.

"This, ladies and gentlemen, is what happens when translocation goes wrong. In your first year you will do nothing more than theory. In the second, meditation techniques. The third you will make tests and experiments. It's not until Year Four we allow you to actually try it. Is that clear?"

Nobody answered. Zeke glanced round at a mass of wide-eyed, pale faces.

"Is that clear?" Knimble demanded again.

"Crystal," Zeke said, and gulped down an urge to vomit.

Chapter Eleven

Psychokinesis 101

The teacher for Psychokinesis 101 was a wobbly old man called Mariner Flounder. The newbies joked the number stood for his age. Damp eyes stared from a forest of wrinkles. His long curls of hair were the colour of dirty snow. Yet Flounder turned out to be Zeke's first major threat.

It happened on the tenth day after their arrival. Flounder was scribbling equations on the plasma-board. The symbols had something to do with brainwaves and atomic mass. The rest was beyond Zeke's understanding. He sat at the back doodling on his magnopad.

Zeke had started to enjoy his deception. Many of his classmates considered themselves special. After all they were humanity's saviours, weren't they? Zeke took satisfaction in fooling them. His satisfaction had settled into complacency, a very dangerous state.

It all changed when Flounder tapped the floor with his stick.

"Time for a demonstration," he announced.

The entire class sat up straight. The instructor began setting up an experiment at the lab bench.

"It's a simple enough stunt," Flounder continued. "I have here a kettle full of H2O, which as we all know means…"

He waited for someone to respond.

"Two atoms of Hydrogen for every one of Oxygen, i.e. common or garden water."

It was Scuff, with one eye on the lesson and the other on a manga book under his desk. Trixie Cutter ran a profitable sideline in pirated comics.

"Exactly, young Bunkum"

"Barnum."

"Quite. So heat the water and the kettle will boil."

He placed it on a fireproof stand.

"We can heat the water by switching the kettle on. But who needs a heat source? As psychokineticists we are able to warm up those molecules mentally. Let me show you."

A hush fell across the classroom as Flounder stared intensely at the kettle. The ticking of the clock seemed louder with every second. All eyes focused on the spout, waiting for a telltale wisp of steam. None came. Flounder sank back into his chair, exhausted.

"Great Orion's Belt, these things get harder as the years slip by," he said, dabbing his sweaty forehead with a hanky.

A chorus of boos rippled across the room. Flounder looked at his class with a helpless expression. "Order, order I say!" But the boos just grew louder. Zeke and Pin-mei exchanged looks.

"Mr Flounder just needs a little time," she whispered.

Zeke nodded. He felt sorry for the old man.

Snod, who was sitting in the next row, turned round.

"That old codger needs retiring."

Snod had developed a cheek the size of Jupiter since joining Trixie's gang.

"No need to be so harsh," Zeke replied.

"Why don't you help him then? You can kiss his boots while you're at it."

"He doesn't need my help," Zeke said quickly, wishing he'd kept quiet.

"Oi, Sir," Snod called out. "Blue boy's volunteering to give you a hand."

"NO!" Zeke hissed at Snod, but it was too late.

"What a capital idea. Come here boy. You with the funny coloured hair."

Flounder waved Zeke to the front. Zeke glanced at Scuff and Pin-mei's horrified expressions. Scuff nodded at him to go. He had no choice.

"What was your name again, boy?"

"Hailey, Sir, Zeke Hailey."

"Right, young man. You're going to heat that water."

"But, Sir! It's forbidden for newbies to use psychic power."

"Tish, tish Bailey. Not with an instructor's supervision."

Zeke scanned through the sea of faces for his friends. Now was the time to put their plan to the test. Could Scuff and Pin-mei cover for him?

"I want you to look at the kettle. Concentrate on the water inside. Imagine the molecules whizzing about."

Zeke pretended to do as he was told. He gazed at the kettle and tensed his brow. Pin-mei's psychokinetic skills were good. Perhaps she could boil the water from the back of the class. He could then claim the credit.

"Focus on those molecules, young Bailey. Take deep, measured breaths. See the molecules. Be the molecules."

Zeke had to make it look good. He closed his eyes and took long gulps of air. He conjured up the image in his mind. Billions of water molecules zinging madly around. At that moment his scalp tingled. His blood pumped faster. He really could see those molecules and they really were getting hotter and hotter.

BOOOOOM!

The screech of ripping plastic blasted his eardrums. A hot tornado threw him to the floor. His eyes opened to a catastrophe of smoke, steam and shell-shocked students.

Principal Lutz kept office on top of the Chasm's highest minaret. Outside the Sun was setting on Mariners Valley. Towering piles of rock were falling into shadow. Their weird, wind bitten shapes reminded Zeke of the monsters in his dreams. He shivered.

Lutz's secretary, Marjorie Barnside, was tapping furiously at her keyboard. She was a stout dour woman with a strong Belfast accent.

"One cold fusion kettle, belonging to the School, destroyed. Five students cut by flying shards of plastic. Two students bruised by falls. One teacher scalded by boiling water." She fixed Zeke with an incriminating glare. "What a shocking waste of school property! Do you have any idea how much those kettles cost?"

Zeke and Pin-mei wriggled under her beady stare. Barnside lowered her head and began typing again.

"Which one of you was it?" Zeke whispered to his friend. Pin-mei had accompanied him to the office after the accident had left him a little shaky.

"Excuse me?"

"Who blew up the kettle? It was Scuff, wasn't it? He has to be the clumsiest psychic in the known universe."

"It wasn't me, Zeke. My thoughts can't reach that far. Not yet."

"I knew it. I'm going to barbecue that overweight yank."

"But it wasn't Scuff either. He swore on his father's millions."

Before Zeke could ask any further questions Lutz's door opened. Three figures emerged and Zeke's jaw dropped. The first was Principal Lutz, the second was Trixie Cutter and the third was Professor Magma. Lutz and Magma warmly shook hands.

"It's been such a pleasure to meet you Professor. *Enchanté!*"

"Oh, call me Tiberius. And I have greatly valued our meeting. Can I say we have an agreement?"

"Totally. I look forward to a long and profitable association. Now young Miss Cutter will escort you back to your vehicle."

Trixie gave Magma a sly wink.

"Right this way, Sir." She pointed to the elevator.

A high-pitched wail pierced the room. Pin-mei had fallen to the floor and was writhing wildly.

"Cushion!" Lutz shouted at Barnside. Lutz lifted off the ground and flew over the chairs cluttering the office. The secretary grabbed a cushion off her seat and threw it into the air. The Principal caught the cushion and landed beside Pin-mei, slipping it under the girl's head.

Zeke's thoughts raced. His best pal was lying on the ground in convulsions. He wanted to do something, but what?

Lutz in contrast, seemed calm and in control. She held onto the girl's arms to prevent any self-injury. Pin-mei continued to struggle, frothing at the mouth. Her eyes lit up like burning magnesium.

"Is it a psychic fit?" Magma asked, arching his eyebrows in disgust.

"Of course, the greater the psychic the greater the fit. This girl must be phenomenally talented," Lutz explained. Magma's eyes twinkled with a greedy gleam.

Lutz wrestled to contain the unconscious girl. Then Pin-mei spoke, but the voice was deep and ghostly.

"It's here! The Spiral's here!"

Zeke's entire body ran cold when he heard those words. His nightmares had spoken of a spiral. But when he glimpsed Professor Magma his blood turned even colder. The shock on the man's face left him in no doubt. Magma recognised that name too.

Chapter Twelve

Scuff's Room

"It's an ill wind," Scuff remarked sagely, crouching over his zombies. He and Zeke were on the floor of his room, separated by a large cube of light. They were in the middle of Scuff's favourite Laserlight game, *Last Zombie Standing*. Little undead holograms stalked a three-dimensional town in search of fresh meat. The idea was to eat as many of the opponent's players as possible. Zeke's *Coven of Dripping Blood* had Scuff's *Oozing Ghouls* on the run.

"An ill wind?" Zeke asked. He wiggled his controller and his zombie-shopkeeper sank its fangs into Scuff's zombie-cop. While Scuff struggled to bring up reinforcements Zeke surveyed his pal's room.

Ten days on Mars and it was already a disaster area. Candy wrappers, toxic underwear, and all manner of debris littered the floor. Textbooks and comics covered the bed. A half-fixed computer with its innards spilling out dominated the desk. Zeke was shocked that a rich kid could be such a slob.

"No, I don't mean my room," Scuff snapped. Zeke wondered again if Scuff was reading his thoughts.

"Pin-mei, taking poorly. Got you off the hook didn't it, bro."

In all the confusion Lutz had dismissed Zeke with a wave of her hand.

"Send the bill to his mother," she instructed Barnside. The Principal then lifted the Chinese girl into her arms and hurried off to the Medical Facility.

"I hope she's okay," Zeke said.

"Some kids get it that way. Fits show exceptional power. You're lucky really, being normal."

"Guess I am," Zeke replied. Somehow he didn't feel particularly fortunate.

"That is if you *are* normal," Scuff added with a funny look.

"What do you mean?"

"Well somebody blew up that classroom, Zeke. And it wasn't me and it wasn't Pin-mei." Scuff pulled on his controller. His zombie-schoolgirl landed a bite on one of Zeke's humans, the pizza-boy. The youth let out an agonising yell and zombified.

"In my powers!" Scuff cackled with his best evil laugh.

The new recruit lumbered off to swell Scuff's horde of cannibals.

"Then there's another mystery. Remember the sycamore and its jammed wings?"

"Remember? My trousers are still in the soak. So?"

"I didn't do it."

"What!"

"I thought I did it, at the time. Sheesh, I wanted to be a hero. But I know in my heart it wasn't me who opened those wings."

Too many emotions bubbled up inside Zeke.

"Rubbish! Total rubbish. Don't mess with me, Scuff," he barked.

"Okey-dokey, bro. Don't get your panties in a twist." Silence fell between them as the holograms battled for superiority.

Zeke focused on steering his putrid pack through the make-believe streets. At length he spoke again. "There's more of that ill wind."

"Oh? You haven't—?"

"I have not! I mean something else happened at Lutz's office."

"What's that, bro?"

"I managed to see through the open door into her study."

"And?"

"Stuffed full of computers. Some real oldies too. The kind that use silicon chips. It must be where they—"

"Keep the records? Well done, Sherlock!"

"Do you think you could hack into them?"

Scuff sighed. "Already tried, bro."

"Hacker proof?"

Scuff raised one eyebrow in disgust. "Zeke! You're looking at the Pan-American Hacking Olympics Champion, 2256, 2257 and 2258. But these computers must be standalone, outside the network. I've been trying for days to infiltrate the Chasm's server, just for you, bro."

"Gosh, thanks. No success?"

"Totally bummed. Not a hint about past students."

"So I'll just have to sneak in when nobody's there."

"With the Chasm's security? Are you totally nuts?"

"What else can I do?"

Scuff twisted his controls. The Oozing Ghouls sprang a surprise attack, rising from the sewers. Zeke's players were caught unawares and quickly devoured.

"That's the fifteenth time you've beaten me."

"You gotta strategise, bro."

Scuff smirked and aimed his remote at his computer station. The glowing cube between them flickered. The blood-splattered streets were replaced with an image of the School. Scuff clicked and zoomed in on the craggy finger of Lutz's minaret. Surveillance and alarms were highlighted in yellow. Both boys studied the system without speaking. Scuff broke the hush.

"The elevator's no good. Wall-to-wall cameras. So the staircase is the only way. But more cameras are installed in the ceiling every twelve feet. Basically as one disappears out of sight another pops up in front of you."

He crawled over to the keyboard and punched up more data.

"That's what I thought. They rotate for a three hundred and sixty degree view. Each rotation lasts ten seconds. You'd have to sprint up the stairs at just the right moment. So each camera is looking away from you."

"As the camera pans round the inside of the staircase I run up the outside? But Scuff, you'd have to be superhuman fast. Can't you just use your psychokinesis to break them?"

Scuff rolled his eyes. "So everyone knows we've broken in? We might as well leave a calling card."

"Couldn't you translocate in?"

"What! Like flying a jet without a single lesson? You want me with a vase coming out my head?"

"Then its useless."

Scuff rubbed his chin. "Now the computerised doors *are* online. I could hack the office door to open in advance. All we have to do is find a way of bounding upstairs faster than humanly possible."

The two friends stared at each other. Scuff was grinning wickedly.

"You've got a strategy, haven't you?" Zeke said, and started grinning himself.

Zeke hesitated at Pin-mei's door. The 'do not disturb' sign was flashing. He pressed the buzzer and smiled into the door-cam.

"Hi, are you there, Pin?"

After a lengthy pause her voice crackled over the intercom. "Yes." She sounded frail.

"I went to the Medical Facility, but Dr. Chandrasar said you were discharged, fully recovered."

"Yes, but on bed rest for a few hours. Sorry, Zeke, I'm not up to visitors."

"No probs."

Another long silence passed.

"Is there anything I can do for you?"

"No, I just need to sleep. Really."

"OK, well, call me if you need me."

Zeke knew he should go but curiosity was burning him up.

"Pin, what did you see? In your premonition?"

"Zeke, I don't want to talk about it."

"But what you said, 'the Spiral is here', what did you mean?"

"It wasn't a premonition. Just a bad dream, about a monster."

"What monster?"

"There was this spiral in the sky, like a black hole. It was sucking people in."

"That was the monster?"

"It came down and sucked up the whole school. It had these terrible eyes, hundreds of bleeding eyes…"

"Pin? Pin-mei?"

"Zeke, I'm really sleepy. See you tomorrow?"

"Okay. I'll pop round after lunch."

"Great. See you. Bye."

The intercom clicked off.

Zeke started to walk away, down the smooth stony passage. He stopped.

That little voice was nagging him from the back of his mind. The same voice he had heard over and over since leaving Earth. Zeke told himself he was being silly and carried on. But the voice kept whispering.

She's in terrible danger!

Chapter Thirteen

Ophir Chasma School Main Corridor Boys' Toilets

"**C**ockroach pills!"

Zeke stared at Scuff's open hand. Half a dozen glossy brown capsules nestled in his palm.

"Shh!" his friend hissed.

They were in the boys' loo, across from the stairway to Lutz's office. Scuff peered through the swing door. It was Sunday morning. Other than a couple of cleanomacs the wing was deserted. The robots slowly trundled along the passage, sweeping up litter with their spinning brush feet.

"The cockroach brain functions seventeen times faster than a human's."

"Oh?" Zeke began. "So that's why they outrun me whenever I try to stomp one?"

"These pills are concentrated cockroach brain chemicals."

Zeke wrinkled his nose. "You're not suggesting we take these?"

"Why not? The military use them in dangerous situations. When they need to get in and out in a hurry."

"No way! I'm not being a human cockroach."

Scuff threw Zeke his 'are-you-nuts' glare. "The pills speed up your reactions, your thought processes. Nothing more. You won't sprout antennae or go scampering under the refrigerator. Klutz!"

Zeke looked unconvinced. "So, we go faster?"

"Now you're getting the plot Einstein. We'll be too fast to see."

"Faster than light?"

"Not that fast! The pills speed our brains up to about ten times normal. Anymore and our synapses would fuse! So what you could do in ten seconds you can do in one. We'll be too fast for the human eye. And if we were caught on camera we'd be just a blur. They only last for four or five minutes, real time, but that's all we need to get up and in."

"And you're sure they're safe?"

"Absolutely!" Scuff insisted, carefully avoiding eye contact.

"How did you get them?"

Scuff flushed.

"Trixie Cutter's black market."

"WHAT! That psychopath!"

"Why not?"

"I don't want a bully like her doing us favours. She'll say we owe her."

Scuff's jaw dropped. "I was trying to help."

Zeke drew a deep breath. Trixie might be an enemy but Scuff was his friend. "How much?"

The tint on Scuff's cheeks deepened. "A couple of thousand Martian."

"Two thousand Martian dollars! Oh Scuff, you shouldn't have!"

"What's the point having a rich father if I can't throw his cash around?"

A guilt attack slapped Zeke in the face. Where would he be without Scuff?

The two boys smiled.

"Here goes then," Zeke said.

Scuff handed him a pill.

"Place it under your tongue and let it dissolve. Watch the clock. You'll know when it's done."

Zeke copied Scuff's actions. He had no idea how a cockroach tasted but he imagined it was similar to the pill. A bitter, nauseating flavour furred up his gums. He gazed at the wall clock.

The time was ten twenty-three. Then it was ten twenty-four. But something was wrong. The second hand was slowing, slower, slower. An intense itchiness tingled the inside of his skull, as if his brain was wriggling its way out. He glanced at his friend. Scuff was starting to flicker. The itchy feeling became unbearable. An urge to crack open his forehead overwhelmed him. Just as a scream began rising in his throat the prickliness ceased. The second hand was at a standstill.

Scuff was in focus again, leaning against a washbasin and grinning like a monkey.

"Hey, bro, do I deliver or do I deliver?"

Zeke pushed at the door but it remained glued in its frame. He turned to Scuff and shrugged his shoulders.

"Inertia and speed differentials, bro. You've pushed it for a nanosecond in real time. Try for longer, but not too much force. At our speed it could ricochet off its hinges."

Zeke and Scuff sauntered lazily over to the foot of the stairs. At first the cleanomacs seemed frozen. Zeke paused for a closer inspection. The robots were moving but too slowly to notice. Zeke clapped his hands with glee. Super speed was exhilarating.

"Don't linger. Ten of our seconds in one spot and we might register on their visual circuits," Scuff said. "Now, there are twenty security cams on the way up. They're all in synch. If we start when the bottom one is facing away we should get to the top."

"Even if we get caught on film we'd only be a blur, right?"

"Sure, bro, but best not to arouse suspicion."

Scuff poked his head around the pillar. "Okay, Camera number one is pointing away. GO! GO! GO!"

Laughing like hyenas the two friends cantered up the stone stairwell. With the security cams as swift as sundials it was easy to dance around them and reach the apex. The door to Barnside's office was waiting for them.

"Open it, bro," Scuff wheezed, exhausted by the sprint. "I reprogrammed the Chasm's security timer to unlock now."

"The technicians in IT told me the School's server was unhackable."

"Yes, Zeke, but they never met a three times under-eighteen champion hacker. Go ahead."

Zeke pushed at the handle. Once again it was surprisingly resistant. They both gripped the handle and tugged. Despite being made of plastic, the door seemed to weigh a ton. The boys grunted as inch by inch it opened. They were in!

"Oh!" Scuff groaned, turning greener than a cabbage. His stomach growled noisily.

"My pill…wearing…off," he said. His voice and movements were winding down. He came to a complete halt. Zeke waved his hand in front of Scuff's eyes. No response. The geek was as still as a waxwork.

Zeke guessed he had only moments before he too decelerated. Wondering if there was anything to do he scrutinized Barnside's office. His gaze alighted on a framed photo on her desk. He bent down for a closer look.

It was a group scene with someone cutting a ribbon. An inscription written in the corner dated the photo as a hundred years old. Zeke studied its details. There, among the crowd, Lutz and Barnside solemnly watched the ceremony.

How could either of them be so old?

At that instant Zeke's stomach quivered violently. A side effect? Scuff's hand began rising, first at a snail's pace, then accelerating. Of course it was not Scuff who was getting faster, but Zeke who was returning to normal.

"Bucket!" Scuff gasped, and they dived for the wastepaper bin...

The sound of Martian plumbing gurgled through the tower.

"Let's hope nobody hears that," Scuff said, as Zeke returned from the toilet with the washed out bin.

Zeke said nothing. He tried the door to Lutz's office. It opened easily. Zeke hesitated for a moment then stepped inside.

"Wow!" Scuff said softly, following on Zeke's heels.

The octagonal shaped room was much larger than Barnside's office. Three galleries, stuffed full of computers and filing cabinets looked down on Lutz's humble work station. Ladders and staircases connected to each level. Fingers of dusty light poked through the skylights.

"Sneaky," Scuff went on. "She has her own independent network. No connection to the Mars-Wide-Web, or even the School's intranet. Watertight security, bro. Bro?"

His friend wasn't listening. Zeke was mesmerised by the artwork behind Lutz' s desk. A large rectangle of rock had been set into the wall.

"What's that? Modern sculpture?"

The ochre slab was engraved with abstract patterns and symbols. A spiral dominated the centre, with all kinds of squiggles and shapes radiating out. A border of dense markings ran around the edge.

"It's Hesperian, you idiot!" Zeke snapped. "A relic. It must be nearly two billion years old."

"How do you know?"

"Believe me, I know."

"Whatever, bro. Time to get busy. Lutz's PC is bound to

connect with the rest of these antiques. I'll hack in from there and do a search for your dad. What's his first name and date of birth?"

Zeke didn't answer.

"Hey, Sigmund, would you mind waking from the trance?"

Zeke continued gazing at the mural. Frustrated, Scuff shoved him.

"Your old man! What was his name and D.O.B.?"

Zeke pulled himself together. "Cole Hailey, born March 12th 2206."

Scuff clicked on the computer and plugged a memory stick into a spare port.

"The very latest in password decoding from the Tokyo underground," he explained with a flush of pride. Zeke had already stopped listening.

"*Dthoth thla ryksi thnga bchrfft xgiishi dthoth thla gleqxuus jchzaa,*" he mumbled, reading aloud the runes in the stone imagery. "All that comes…out of the dangerous pattern…no, dangerous spiral…eats up space.. and…everybody….dies."

The image rippled. Something was happening. Zeke had activated something when he voiced those ancient syllables.

The picture was growing. And the rest of the room was shrinking. Within a few seconds Lutz's office, along with Scuff tapping away at her keyboard, disappeared beneath the rock frame.

Zeke put out a foot and stepped into a two-dimensional world.

Chapter Fourteen

Inside the picture

Zeke held up his hands and saw circles and rectangles. He had changed from flesh and bone to a line diagram. Fear swamped him.

"Don't panic," he said, gritting his teeth, only to realise he didn't have any teeth.

Thoughts crowded his head. The engraving had to be some kind of Hesperian technology, similar to Magma's orb. But what was it doing to him? Could he die inside this picture, or worse, become trapped forever?

"I said don't panic."

Surely it was an illusion. And if it was all in his mind he couldn't come to any harm. The important thing was to explore deeper. The answers to everything that was happening might lay ahead. Zeke steeled himself and put forward an elliptical foot.

Above and beneath him were segmented hexagons, each with six external lines serving as limbs. Instinct told him these were the long dead Hesperians.

"What kind of creatures were you? Octopi? Crabs?"

They were screaming. Their bodies trembled as they desperately scuttled away. Zeke glanced higher. A giant black spiral dominated the flat sky, rotating and expanding. As it increased it was eating into tall triangular mountains. Smaller spirals sprouted from its central ravenous tentacle.

"DON'T LOOK!" the Hesperians shrieked in Martian, as they scurried past. But it was too compelling to turn away. Zeke watched as the slower hexagons were sucked up into the Spiral's fanged curves. Blood rained.

And yet as Zeke watched, his sense of horror gave way to a strange feeling. *A curiosity.*

How must it feel to be snatched up into the sky and devoured? To feel bones cracking beneath those building-sized teeth? A memory popped into his mind. A nasty scab on the knee sustained during sports practice. He remembered the sense of relief as he peeled the dried clot away. Perhaps entering the Spiral was like that?

Zeke's fascination grew. He could become bigger and better than an insignificant human. Merge with the beautiful darkness. A thrill shuddered his body.

"Digest me! Over here!" he cried with a sudden joy, waving energetically.

His tiny inner voice interrupted.

'Think you fool! THINK!'

Zeke shook his stick-figure head. He was in a tug of war between the Spiral and the voice. But the Spiral was stronger. For the first time Zeke felt its great wind, pulling him nearer. Terror broke the spell.

"THIS ISN'T REAL!" he bellowed with all his might.

The two-dimensional world freeze-framed. A Martian word slithered up to him. He spelled out its five runes.

"*Thrith, Dthoth, shfah, nthrth, nxngth.*"

That spelt *nbqchii* or in English 'ask'. Zeke no longer marvelled at his fluency in a primeval alien language. The orb had re-programmed his brain to understand. That much was obvious. But what use was the orb to Magma?

The word shuffled impatiently. ASK!

Zeke struggled to pronounce a question. The non-human syllables had his Earth tongue in knots.

"What is this place?"

The letters rearranged themselves.

'A warning.'

"I don't understand. Is this what happened to you?"

The word became a sentence.

'Will happen to you.'

"What will happen to us?" Zeke demanded, the Martian syllables clinging to his palette.

It jumbled and un-jumbled.

'Key unlocks Infinity Trap.'

"Make sense!" he barked. Confusion gushed through his brain.

The words didn't move. Zeke frantically tried to think. He knew he had to ask the right questions, but what were they?

"How can I stop this happening?"

'Save her.'

Save who? What was the picture trying to tell him?

"Zeke. Zeke?"

He glanced over his shoulder. Scuff's face was creased with worry.

"Mars calling planet Zeke, are you receiving me?"

Zeke was standing infront of the prehistoric engraving. He had never left Lutz's office.

"Scuff! Have you seen Pin-mei today?" Zeke demanded, grabbing his friend hard.

"I've found the data. Your dad's file."

"THAT'S NOT IMPORTANT. TELL ME ABOUT PIN."

Scuff gazed at him in disbelief.

"Not important? After all I've risked—"

"Tell me what you know!"

"About Pin? What's to tell? She popped in this morning. Feeling much better."

"Where is she?"

"Cycling, bro. Trixie Cutter invited her on a cross-country tour of the Valley with Snod."

"WHAT!" Zeke shouted. "GIVE ME THE PILLS!"

Bewildered, Scuff handed three of the four remaining tablets. Zeke dashed for the door, swallowing down all of them. Scuff lurched after him.

"Don't take them all! It could be fatal!"

"No time!"

"WAIT. THEY MUST TAKE EFFECT. THE CAMERAS WILL SEE YOU."

But Zeke no longer cared. He threw Scuff aside and sprinted for the stairs. Scuff watched him go before gulping down the last pill.

"You are so totally over, bro, finito."

Zeke flew down the stone steps three at a time. All twenty security cams he dodged on the way up caught him on the descent. He didn't care. Pin-mei was in danger, he knew it.

The cockroach pills didn't kick in until he reached the ground floor and was already racing to the main door. His chest boiled. His heart boomed like an engine. His skin squirmed. He ran faster and faster, zooming past waxworks that were really people.

"I must get to the bike. I must, I must," he cried. He was going so quickly the school corridors blurred into one.

And then he was there, beside his mountain bike in the parking lot. How had he arrived? The last few moments were a blank. But there was no time to think about it. Zeke jumped onto his bike and peddled furiously out, through the open entrance, into the vast bowl of Ophir Chasma.

Which way? Mountain biking was a popular pastime among students. Fresh tracks in the sand indicated several bicycles had gone out and back already. Pulling at his blue hair he scoured the dirt. A set of three trails headed off to a distant ravine. They had not returned.

Zeke turned the handlebars and pushed off in the same direction, his wheels humming under the pressure of super-speed. He shot across the barren scene. The rocks gave way to boulders. The trail threaded into a fissure. Sharp crags rose up on all sides like clawing hands.

He turned a corner and cycled headlong into Cutter and Snod. From his super-speed perspective they were travelling as fast as slugs. Cutter wore an expression of malevolent glee. Snod's face told a different story. He was terrified.

Zeke rode on, deeper into the gorge.

A convulsion punched through his stomach, throwing him from the bike. The pills were wearing off. He vomited into the red dust. With tears of pain he forced himself to his feet and remounted. He had to find Pin-mei.

Now Zeke was back in real time he considered switching Albie on. But that would slow him down. He pressed on, struggling to maintain his balance as the pills' after effects rumbled around his guts.

"HELP!"

The scream bounced off the basalt cliffs. She was somewhere up ahead. There was another sound too, the moaning of wind. Zeke grunted and rammed down hard on his pedals.

The last bend opened up onto the plains of Mariners Valley.

"What on Mars!"

In the distance his friend was cycling for her life. A dust devil, larger than a fully grown man, seemed to be pursuing her.

"PIN-MEI!" he shouted, but she couldn't hear.

It was gaining on her. Zeke's blood froze. Within the whirlwind he could make out a white light in the shape of a man. It appeared to be walking leisurely but every step crossed several metres.

With a sudden leap the dust devil engulfed Pin-mei in a torrent of dust. An impenetrable cloud obscured them both. A moment later her bike hurtled through the air and crashed behind Zeke.

"PIN-MEI!" he shrieked again. Leaping back onto his saddle he zoomed after the swirling column. But it was retreating at an impossible rate and melted into the ochre landscape.

"PIN-MEI" he cried, desperately searching the horizon. His voice echoed back across miles of dead rock. The sand slowly settled and the crushing silence returned. Pin-mei was gone.

Part Two

Chapter Fifteen

Lutz's Office

Principal Lutz buried her face in her hands. Zeke sat in front of her desk staring at the clock on the wall. He listened as it ticked away the seconds, like a time bomb counting down to an explosion. And then came the BOOM!

The Principal erupted in a blast of foul language. Zeke turned beetroot-red as the words slammed into him. Lutz's outburst leapt from English to German to Russian. Zeke looked out the window at the skeletal fingers of rock and said nothing. Finally the Principal ran out of curses and sat back down.

"Never in all my years running this establishment—and believe me they are many—have I experienced such criminal behaviour."

Zeke remained mute.

"First you break into my office. Do you deny it?

Zeke shook his head. The woman aimed her remote and clicked. A tiny hologram appeared on her desk, replaying the security cam footage. Zeke was running down the steps again and again.

"And can you explain, *mein kleiner Einbrecher*, how you evaded the detection all the way up? But flaunted your presence on the way down?"

"Translocation Ma'am," Zeke fibbed bravely.

Lutz drew a long breath.

"Which is forbidden to first years, along with all other forms of psychic behaviour. But I can scarcely credit a mere boy of fifteen capable of thinking himself up a hundred and fifty feet. Stick out your tongue!"

Startled, Zeke obeyed.

"Aha!" Lutz cried. "A pallid, greenish tongue, blood shot eyes, and," she sniffed loudly, "a hint of malodorous sweat."

Zeke blushed deeper. Did he stink?

"Cockroach pills! Only available through the black market. So we have breaking and entering, racketeering, lying. Do you wish to declare any other offences?"

Zeke took a long gulp.

"With respect, Ma'am, you can expel me as many times as you wish later on—"

Lutz jumped to her feet. "HOW DARE YOU TAKE THAT TONE WITH ME!"

"But Ma'am, right now Pin's life is in danger."

"I AM COMING TO THAT, BOY!"

Another silence. Lutz struggled to regain her composure.

"And the greatest of all your crimes. Kidnapping! Will you confess your part in this villainy."

Zeke was dumbfounded. She was accusing him?

"Principal Lutz! I'm the one who reported it. I'm her friend."

She smiled scornfully and pointed to the ancient Martian engraving on the wall behind her.

"Oh that's right. My only indulgence over the long years spent in this godforsaken backwater, my treasure, issued you a prophecy!"

"I know it sounds crazy, Ma'am, but it's true. It's more than a picture, it's some kind of mechanism."

"STOP! Every Hesperian artefact is rigorously examined by our best scientists. If it were anything other than an old carving we'd know. So don't insult me with your science fiction. Have the decency to own up."

Zeke's tears were building. He forced them back.

"Everything I said is true. The picture did come alive. I did step into it. And Pin was abducted by a dust devil."

Lutz banged her fist down on the desk.

"LIES, LIES, LIES!"

"Why don't you ask Trixie Cutter? What was she doing there?"

"More slander? Bad mouthing one of our finest students. Head of her year, straight A grades, exemplary conduct. How low will you stoop, Hailey?"

"She and Snod are involved in this."

"She and Snod were searching for Pin-mei. I won't hear any more false accusations from you."

Zeke burned with the unfairness of it all. But he bit back the words he was yearning to say. Perhaps Lutz was in on the conspiracy?

"May I ask what's being done to find Pin?"

"The crime has been reported to the Governor's Office. He has dispatched his Lieutenant In Chief from Tithonium Central. He'll be here by morning and no doubt will deal with you. In the meantime our best remote viewers are in deep meditation. If anyone can locate the unfortunate waif they can."

"I know exactly where she is. Professor Magma is behind all this. I know it."

"DESIST!" Lutz shrieked. "I will not have you dragging persons of good honour into this scandal. That man is a reputable academic, recent benefactor to this school and, much to our good luck, a newly recruited lecturer. Tomorrow night he's presenting a slideshow on his Martian digs. A good dose of science will cheer up all those Earth-sick newbies pining for their parents."

Zeke could contain the tears no longer. They streamed down his cheeks.

"That won't work on me, boy. Generations of duplicitous boys have tried and failed to find my soft spot. Sadly for you it's a Martian quicksand."

Lutz paused. When she next spoke her voice was softer.

"Tell me now, Hailey. Where is she?"

"Look," he replied, wiping his eyes. "I broke into your office. I've admitted that. I wanted to see my father's file. Yes I used cockroach pills. I didn't bother with them on the way down as, believe me or not, I had a premonition. I was trying to save her. Honestly."

A crafty look crept across Lutz's wide features.

"Then answer me this, young Hailey. Did you break in alone, or did you have an accomplice?"

That was the last question Zeke wanted to answer. How could he incriminate Scuff? Luckily bluffing his way into the greatest school in the Solar System had given Zeke plenty of practice at lying. He looked the Principal straight in the eye.

"I acted alone, Ma'am. I promise."

She leaned back, satisfied with his answer.

"Young Hailey you have been a troublemaker from the moment you fell from the skies. At the very least you will be drummed out of the school. If you are lucky you will be translocated Earthside to a reform school. Unlucky and you'll be imprisoned at the Tithonium Detention Facility. Until the Lieutenant arrives you are confined to quarters. DO NOT step outside your room. *Comprendez-vous?*"

"Yes, Ma'am."

Silence.

"So, Ma'am, could I possibly see my father's file?"

"GET OUT OF MY SIGHT BEFORE I HAVE YOU VAPORISED!"

Chapter Sixteen

Zeke's Cave

I t was the day after the interrogation with Lutz. Zeke was lying on his bed staring at the pitted ceiling of his cave. Images of his father and Pin-mei danced through his brain. Should he postpone the hunt for his father in favour of his friend? Would his father understand?

Zeke was also puzzled by Scuff's absence. His friend had neither visited nor returned any messages. He couldn't understand why.

There was a knock on the door. At last!

"Scuff? Is that you?"

The door opened. It was not Scuff, but a broad-shouldered man in rust-coloured military fatigues. Zeke noticed immediately the stranger's waxed moustache, wicked grin and twinkling eyes.

"Lieutenant Doughty at your service, young man," he said, and bowed.

Lost for words Zeke boiled up some tea with the cold-fusion kettle. The Lieutenant made himself at home, pushing his huge frame into the old armchair.

"Don't suppose you've any biscuits? Tea's a bit too wet without one." He smirked, sipping noisily from his mug. Zeke was taken aback. The last thing he expected from the Governor's representative was a cosy chat. Doughty read the confusion on Zeke's face.

"Now lets get one thing straight. I'm on your side. A man's innocent until proven guilty, isn't he?"

"Absolutely," Zeke beamed.

"I told that Principal woman, I said, look lady, I'm in charge of this case and you'll do as I say. And as for that young man you've got stowed below decks, as far as I'm concerned he's only a witness at this stage of the proceedings."

"Oh thank you, Sir, I mean, Lieutenant."

"Call me Leo. Short for Leopold."

"Thanks, um, Leo. What happens now?"

"His flaming Lordship the Governor-of-Mars has entrusted ten soldiers to my command. They're out scouring Ophir Chasma for any clues to this young girlie's whereabouts. None of this namby-pamby remote viewing nonsense. Your teachers might have faith in it but I prefer more old-fashioned methods of detection. In the meantime I will be conducting my-er-research, in the school."

"But I know who the guilty party is. It's that madman Magma."

"Guilty is he? Can you prove that in a court of law? Anyway if you're so convinced he did the dirty deed, you can help me interview him tonight after his lecture. I've never met the man, so I'd be grateful of your assistance."

"Really? That's great!" Zeke cried. "You do believe my story, don't you, about the Dust Devil?"

"Dust Devil? First time I've heard one of them listed as a suspect. No, seems more likely your eyes were playing tricks. But I'll keep an open mind. If there are any devil winds out there kidnapping the citizens of Mars they'll have me to contend with."

"What about me? Am I—"

"Free to go? Back to class as if nothing ever happened. In fact you can be my eyes. Sort of undercover junior agent kind of thingy."

"Yes please!"

Doughty offered his hand and they shook. Zeke tried hard not to wince as the big beefy man crushed his palm.

Zeke buzzed Scuff's doorbell for the fourth time. The 'at home' light was on. So why wasn't the Canadian answering?

"Finally!"

The door opened to reveal the spots and spiky hair of Jasper Snod.

"What are you doing here?" Zeke exclaimed.

"None of yours, freaky," Snod replied tapping his long skinny nose. "Now hop it."

"Scuff? Scuff?" Zeke called, peering over the boy's shoulder. He could see Scuff's back, hunched over his computer station. Apparently Scuff had no desire to greet his best pal. As Snod reached for the close button Zeke grabbed his arm.

"You know what's going on, don't you. With Pin-Mei, Magma, the Dust Devil. Just tell me and I'll help you. Please!"

Their eyes met. For a split-second Snod's face wavered. But this brief lapse disappeared beneath an angry scowl.

"You really are nuts," Snod said with a curled lip. He pushed Zeke back outside and the door slid between them.

When Zeke arrived a few minutes early the auditorium was almost full. Every student in the school wanted to know about the ancient Martians. He spied Scuff in a far corner with Snod and a couple of Cutter's goons. He waved but Scuff deliberately looked away. Lieutenant Doughty stood at the back while the Mariners were taking their seats in the upper gallery.

The curtains raised and Magma's gaunt figure strode onto the stage.

"Boys, girls and Mariners, let me thank you for inviting me here today. I can promise you a most enthralling account of my life and work."

He clicked the remote and the first holo-slide appeared, hovering in the air. A little boy was digging sandcastles on a beach.

"My love of archaeology began many years ago..."

Time crawled like a dying snail. Magma's talk meandered through his life. Clearly he had two passions, archaeology and Tiberius Magma. The audience began dozing off. Some sneaked out whenever the Professor turned away. The older students used their psychic skills to escape. Several boys in the front row blurred and vanished.

Yet Magma droned on about ruins and lifetime achievement awards.

"Professor, what about the Martians?" Zeke called out, unable to bear another moment of the man's vanity.

Magma threw him a curious look.

"Yes, well, what a lot they have to offer us."

The remote clicked. A picture of the Martian landscape materialised. And then another and another, dreary views of nothing, a mud heap here, a hole in the ground there.

"Most discoveries have been found in the Noctis Labyrinthis, which is why I have my dig there. The name is Latin for night maze. Imagine a network of criss-crossing ravines, a staggering five miles high, but rarely more than a few feet wide. Too deep to catch the sunlight. A man could loose his way in there. Forever!"

Zeke raised a hand.

"Sir, what can you tell us about the Martian artefacts? The orbs for instance?

Magma smiled maliciously.

"Useless lumps of rock of no interest whatsoever."

Zeke sat back in his chair. The man was lying. Perhaps Magma had come to the school deliberately to cover his tracks. But there was no point trying to get at the truth. Zeke decided to stay quiet.

The presentation dragged on. The professor explained about the three geological ages of Mars, the Noachian, the Hesperian, and lastly the Amazonian. The first was an era of chaos, with oceans of lava and meteor storms. The second was Mars' most Earth-like period, when water flowed and life evolved. Then something happened, turning that watery world into a dry, airless wasteland.

"Why did Mars change?" somebody asked at the front. It was Scuff.

Magma smiled back. "Oh, we're nowhere near solving that puzzle, young man."

More deception, Zeke thought. Some cataclysm destroyed the Hesperians, something to do with the Spiral, whatever that was. And Magma knew everything. Zeke could see it in his eyes.

Somebody coughed in the gallery. It was Lutz.

"Forgive me interrupting, Professor Magma, but time is against us. I must reluctantly ask you to draw your, um, fascinating lecture to an end."

"It's been a pleasure."

"Let's show our appreciation, shall we," Lutz said. A half-hearted round of applause lasted for a few seconds before the spectators hurried from the hall.

Lieutenant Doughty forced his way against the tide of people. As he reached Zeke he bent over and whispered, "Come on! Let's make that old scoundrel sing like a canary."

Chapter Seventeen

The Auditorium

Doughty bounded up the steps onto the stage, with Zeke at his heels.

"Professor Magma, not so fast."

Magma was tidying up his notes.

"Ah! Lieutenant Doughty. How can I help you?"

Doughty reddened with anger. "You can help a whole lot Professor. With the disappearance of a student from this school. The Chinese girl."

"Ah yes. I saw the missing posters on my way in. How terribly distressing."

"TELL US WHERE SHE IS!" Zeke bellowed, boiling with frustration.

"HAILEY!"

Zeke and Doughty spun round. Principal Lutz was standing where a moment before there was no one. She glared at Zeke.

"How dare you speak so insolently to a guest of my school."

She said to Doughty, "Lieutenant, may I remind you the students take their orders from *me*."

"And may I remind you, Madam, that as a representative of the Governor of Mars my powers exceed yours."

"Lieutenant, I wish to speak to you in private. This way," Lutz snapped, and strode off the stage.

Doughty sauntered after her. "Zeke, keep an eye on the suspect. I won't be long."

Zeke was speechless. Quite unexpectedly he was alone with Magma. Zeke turned and faced the man's alligator smile. Zeke gulped.

"Well we find ourselves at a bit of an impasse boy, don't we?" the Professor grinned. "Let's drop the little charade. In fact I want you to help me."

"Never!"

"Are you so sure, boy? Wouldn't you like to see another artefact?"

"What?"

Magma licked his lips.

"The Martian artefacts you were curious about earlier. I must say you were the only one paying attention. That deserves a reward."

Zeke bit his lip. What was Magma playing at?

"There are indeed five Martian artefacts. Four are secretly gathering dust on Earth, except, ahem, I borrowed one. I call it The Orb of Words. But you know all about that, don't you?"

"I haven't a clue what you're on about," Zeke replied.

With a sudden movement the Professor flicked a note card at him. Zeke instinctively caught it. One side was covered in Martian scrawl.

"*Thvrygsh zhhahoo gfeechi mneu,*" Zeke read aloud without thinking. Then his face coloured.

"You're evil! Evil!" he shouted.

Magma gurgled in delight. "You see we both know what that means. 'Little girl is my prisoner'."

"Except you've spelt 'girl' wrong, and used a verb where you needed a noun."

"Oh bravo! A grasp of Hesperian years ahead of mine. How very useful."

"I'm going to tell on you. I'll make them believe me."

"Oh, I seriously doubt that. Nobody's going to believe a child. How old are you? Ah yes. *I'm fifteen, not a little boy.*" Magma said the last sentence in a baby voice.

Zeke clenched his teeth, but said nothing.

"We've gone off the subject. Don't you want to know about the fifth orb? I can show it to you right now. It's in the side room."

Magma beckoned Zeke to follow. Zeke scanned the auditorium for a sign of Doughty or one of the Mariners. The hall was deserted.

Magma was springing some kind of trap. Zeke could see that, but as long as the madman had Pin-mei he had to play along. Any risk was worth it to save her.

"Okay, I'm coming."

Magma walked briskly across the stage and through the side door. Zeke shadowed him inside. They were in a small room where Magma had prepared his talk. A leather case rested on a table.

"Go on, open it." Magma beamed.

"No, you."

"Tsk, tsk, are all today's youngsters so suspicious?"

Magma lifted the top. There was an orb inside, but not the one from the Televator. This one was orangey-red, as smooth and shiny as marble and without any markings.

Zeke gasped sharply. It was beautiful, more beautiful than the Orb of Words. An odd desire overwhelmed him. Its sheen and subtle colouring was crying out to be touched. The little voice inside his head whispered, 'don't', but Zeke ignored it. He reached out a finger.

The moment he made contact he knew it was a mistake. The orb expanded at phenomenal speed. In an instant it was the size of a house and still growing. Zeke's finger had fused to the surface. He was yanked upwards, dangling against its glossy side as it exploded. After ten seconds it was as huge as a city. Twenty seconds and bigger than a country. It stopped after thirty seconds. The orb was now a planet.

Zeke lay on its ground, forcing slow deep breaths into his lungs. The nausea ebbed away. He stood up shakily and looked around, feeling light-headed in the Orb's low gravity. The orange plain radiated away in all directions, flat and gleaming. Nothing disturbed its pristine condition, not a hill, not a ridge, not a single scratch. This was a perfectly formed world.

"Oh no!" he groaned, clutching his scrambled guts. The orb hadn't inflated into a planetary body. It was him. He had shrunk to microscopic dimensions!

Sure enough, what passed for a sun was really the room's photon lamp. The sky was square and white with four colossal corners. Zeke was looking at the ceiling. Beneath the square the sky turned woody yellow, the walls.

With sickening speed a celestial object filled the heavens. Zeke felt a flash of fear. The great shape in the sky paused. It was Magma.

Zeke remembered his dreams, of giant monsters stomping across landscapes. This was far worse. Magma was on a scale way beyond that, with a head larger than any moon. His shoulders and chest dropped beyond the horizon. He was wearing an electron-microscope eyepiece, obviously to see Zeke. The antenna attached to the earpiece was probably a micro-sound receiver. This meant Magma could also hear him.

The giant moved nearer eclipsing the electric sun and plunging the Orb-world into shadow. Magma's lips were speaking. His words rolled across the perfect plain like thunder.

"Well, I certainly cut you down to size!" The immense head cackled.

Zeke scanned his surroundings. He felt horribly vulnerable, with nowhere to run, nothing to give cover. At any moment Magma could reach down with his colossal thumb and squash an area the size of England.

Chapter Eighteen

On a Small World

"I call this one the Orb of Can Do," Magma boomed. "Because I can do this."

He pursed his lips and blew across the surface of the orb-planet. A gale rose in the distance and howled towards Zeke. Before he could run the wind tumbled him to the floor. He skidded along the shiny-smooth surface by the seat of his trousers, choking on Magma's bad breath. The storm of halitosis faded as quickly as it came.

Zeke stood up, unsteady and scared.

"Or this!"

Magma tossed a one-dollar coin. It spun across the sky like a flattened moon and crashed out of sight. The shockwaves threw Zeke back onto the ground.

"How about this one?"

The archaeologist dragged his fingernails down the side of the orb. The high-pitched sound screeched into Zeke's eardrums.

"I could play this game all day," the gigantic face smirked. "But duty calls, sadly."

Magma moved away, out of focus. He returned and held up a note card the size of Africa.

"Mr Hailey, translate this Hesperian and I'll free you and your little girlfriend. Space Scout's honour."

"I don't believe you."

Magma brought the card nearer to the planet. Zeke recognised the words although they were too cryptic to make sense.

The key is a brain, for thoughts alone unlock the Infinity Trap.

"Come on my little blue-headed boy, tell me."

"What do you need me for? You translate it."

"I told you already. You're fluent. Compared to you, Earth's brainiest linguists are moronic beginners. I know the passage is about the Infinity Trap but no more. NOW TELL ME!"

Magma's raised voice caused the tiny landscape to tremble.

"Why don't you use the Orb of Words on yourself? Afraid?"

"You're even more stupid than I suspected. I'm not psychic. The orbs only work on psychics. The Hesperians had great intelligence way ahead of Man's current stage of evolution. Only Psychics have brainwaves sophisticated enough to trigger the Hesperian technology."

Zeke was dumbfounded. He was about to tell the Professor he wasn't psychic when he realised there was no point. But how had two orbs worked on him? Magma must be wrong. Still perhaps it was better the archaeologist didn't know that.

A sudden earthquake shook Zeke off his feet once again. Magma was rocking the Orb case.

"Wakey, wakey! Tell me what I need to know."

"And then you'll kill me! What's the point?"

Magma stamped his foot, the impact reverberating like a sonic boom.

"You WILL tell me—oh drat. Someone's at the door."

He flipped the case lid and night fell in a straight line. Zeke sat in the starless dark and desperately reviewed his options. There didn't seem to be any.

"What was that?"

Faraway in the blackness something was making a scratching noise. Faraway but getting closer. It sounded like feet, lots of feet, scampering in Zeke's direction. A horrible thought occurred to him. Maybe he wasn't alone on this planet? Hadn't the archaeologist said the Orb was gathering dust for years back on Earth? Supposing it had gathered microscopic dust-mites as well? Dust mites were hardly psychic, so they wouldn't have shrunk. Didn't they feed off discarded skin cells? And what was he now but a skin cell?

Fear clawed at Zeke's throat. But then a new day dawned. A wall of daylight zoomed up from the horizon. Zeke was almost glad to see Magma's vast face.

"That policeman friend of yours is being most annoying. Says I won't be allowed out of this horrid school until you've turned up. I have no choice but to let you go."

Magma had a malicious twinkle in his eyes as he spoke. Strangely, Zeke fancied there was something more Magma was keeping to himself. But Zeke was in no position to argue.

"Actually you could escape at any time. Just jump," Magma went on.

Zeke immediately leapt six feet. With the Orb's weak gravity it was easy, but nothing happened.

"Try harder," Magma said.

Zeke summoned all his strength and kicked off. Six feet, ten feet, fifteen feet, he felt himself flying upwards. He looked back to see the glossy ground falling away. The horizon curved. The landscape became a circle, as big as a continent, but rapidly shrinking. Zeke flew higher. The Orb-world became smaller and smaller. Above him the square sky was contracting inwards. Magma was reducing to his normal height.

And it was over. Zeke was back in the side room, next to the table. The Orb was no larger than a football.

"Tell anyone about this and the girl ends up in a shallow Martian grave," Magma said through a leering smile.

There was something in his hand. A gun! He aimed it at Zeke.

"Nooooooo—"

Zeke felt as if a trillion volts had zapped his brain. He opened his eyes. It took a moment to focus. He was in his room! He tried to speak but his tongue was glued to the roof of his mouth.

"Take it easy, kiddo."

It was Lieutenant Doughty, mug of tea in one hand and a glass of water in the other. He handed Zeke the water, grinning ear to ear.

"Was it one of those psychic fits?" he asked.

"What?" Zeke replied, rubbing his sore head.

"I found you on the stage. What knocked you out? A psychic fit?"

"Magma shot me. You've got to arrest him. He admitted he's got Pin-mei."

"Hold your horses, cowboy, what do you mean you were shot? Where's the bullet hole?"

Zeke quickly ran his hands up and down his body. Apart from a hurricane force headache he was fine.

"It must have been one of those guns the police use. At least they do on Earth."

"You mean a neural disruptor. We have them here too. Wipe out the old synapses long enough to cause unconsciousness but no serious damage. You're saying Magma used one on you?"

"Totally!"

"You'd better start at the beginning."

In between sips of water Zeke poured out the whole incredible story. Magma's confession, the Orb of Can-Do, the note card in Hesperian runes.

"Hesperian writing? And you understood it? Amazing!"

The Lieutenant pulled his magnopad from his briefcase and began taking notes.

"This is very important, Zeke. Tell me exactly what it said."

"The key is a brain, for thoughts alone unlock the Infinity Trap."

Doughty scribbled furiously.

"Are you sure that's what it said? Absolutely?"

"Yes, Leo. But what does it mean?"

"Haven't the foggiest old bean. But I need to bring this to the Governor's attention a.s.a.p.."

"But you are going to Magma's dig? You've got to. He's holding Pin-mei."

"I can't do anything until I get a warrant from the Governor. That's why I need to present him this evidence. Hopefully I can persuade him to act."

Zeke was distraught.

"You're not…leaving me?"

Leopold Doughty looked him in the eye.

"Listen, boy. Saving your little friend is my top priority. But I have to act within the law. Can't go storming into Magma's camp guns blazing. Now have faith. I know it's tough for you here, but stay put and keep an eye on what's going on. I'll be back in a few days and we'll take it from there."

A few days! Zeke wanted to rush out into Mariners Valley right now. The policeman saw the disappointment on Zeke's face and ruffled his hair.

"Well, better go, old chap. Sooner I leave the sooner I return. I have to take my squad back with me too. Now chin up."

The huge man squeezed himself through the door to Zeke's cave and was gone. Zeke fell back against his mattress, sinking in an ocean of depression. Pin-mei had been gone three days. At least he knew she was alive, but for how long? He missed her terribly. In fact he was missing a lot of people, Pin-mei, his mother, Scuff, even Doughty who had only been gone two minutes.

Zeke curled up in a ball.

"I've got to do something. I've got to do something," he repeated over and over, long into the Martian night.

Chapter Nineteen

The Cranny

Zeke sat alone, poking two Martian sausages with his fork. How he yearned for his mum's egg and bacon. But even more he yearned for her smile. He glanced around at the other sleepy students, yawning over their cold fry-ups. Everyone was ignoring him.

"Finished, Sir?" droned a dishwashomac.

"No, not yet."

"Very good, Sir," the robot said, stacking dirty plates inside its cube-shaped body. It closed the flap. The sound of whooshing water rumbled inside its belly.

Two lanky girls in Zeke's year strolled over with their trays full of food. They threw Zeke poisonous looks and sat nearby. Although Zeke was free he was still Suspect Number One as far as his co-students were concerned.

"Here," Zeke said, pushing his uneaten meal towards the mac. He couldn't face food this morning. At that moment the ketchup bottle levitated off Zeke's table and glided over to the next.

"You've got a nerve. Stuffing food down like nothing's happened," one of the girls called over, plucking the ketchup from midair. Zeke groaned.

"What?" he asked after a long pause.

"Don't 'what' us. You know full well. The disappearance. You had a hand in it, didn't you?"

"I was not involved in Pin-mei's disappearance."

"Don't play innocent. We're not talking about her. We mean Jimmy Swallow!"

Zeke's face clouded with confusion. Jimmy Swallow was a senior, top of his class at remote viewing and captain of the school basketball team.

"Door to his room found wide open this morning and no sign of him. Somebody broke in through the fire exit. Lutz is hopping mad."

Without another word, Zeke leapt up and dashed from the cafeteria.

"See, guilty as hell," one girl chirped, and stabbed at her sausage.

When Zeke reached Swallow's room in South Wing, he found one Mariner standing guard and several more inside searching for clues. Zeke knew they were wasting their time.

He crouched down. Sure enough there it was. A telltale trail of ochre sand! Zeke stood up and followed its track. It led straight to the nearest fire exit and down the outer escape, where it merged into the Martian soil.

The Dust Devil had sneaked into school and made off with another victim. Zeke had no doubt it was all part of Magma's plot. But why kidnap another student? And were Jimmy and Pin-mei chosen on purpose or merely in the wrong place at the wrong time?

A hundred voices crowded his head.

Zeke had come to Mars searching for his father. But now Pin-mei was missing and nobody seemed to be lifting a finger to help. He remembered the night they arrived. He'd promised to look after her, to be her Martian big brother. He couldn't let her down. His father had vanished years ago, somewhere unbelievably far away. The Chinese girl had vanished right now, right here on Mars. And she was in terrible danger.

"I can't wait any longer," Zeke muttered, and clenched his fists.

Zeke moved a few electrobooks down from the shelf and peered through the gap. He had a perfect view of his ex-friend, sitting alone at a workstation. Zeke gulped and walked out into the soft light of the school library.

"Hi," he said, taking a seat.

Silence.

"So, you're not speaking to me?"

Scuff glared at him, eyes wide with scorn.

"Look Scuff, I'm sorry, really, really sorry about leaving you in Lutz's office. Don't you see? I had to save Pin."

"If you saved her where is she then?"

"You don't think I'm involved in these abductions, do you?"

"There's a lot that think you are. Teachers and students."

"And what do you think?"

Scuff frowned. "That you're a user and a liar. After all, you cheated your butt off to get here. Who knows what you're capable of!"

Zeke was too stunned to speak. Why was Scuff reacting like this? What had Trixie Cutter said to him? A lump began forming in Zeke's throat. Their friendship was truly dead.

"Listen. I'm going tonight."

"Going?"

"To the Noctis Labyrinthis—"

"Magma's dig? You're still harping on about that old coot? Trixie says he's as sweet as a Cherry Crater chocolate."

"Right, Trixie the school psychopath. Since when was she an authority on good character?"

"Whatever, bro."

"Finally. I'm your bro again."

"Slip of the tongue, you're no brother of mine."

"I'm that evil?"

"You're that stupid. The Noctis Labyrinthis must be a thousand miles away. And you're going to peddle it?"

Scuff chuckled coldly. Zeke flushed. He hadn't realised how far it was.

"I'll borrow a Glow-Worm from one of the Mariners."

The Glow-Worm brand of scooters were very popular among the teachers. Their rechargeable engines could be powered, not only by solar power, but any light source, even starlight. They came specifically designed for the Martian environment, with spherical wheels, super-shock absorbers and survival gear.

"Steal, you mean. Why don't you go the whole hog and make off with the School Millipede." Scuff couldn't stop laughing.

A moment ago Zeke had been close to tears. Now he wanted to punch his former friend in his piggy face.

"No, a Glow-Worm will do just fine. I can stop at Yuri-Gagarin Freetown, then Tithonium Central to stock up on food. Shouldn't take more than, um, four days."

Scuff guffawed so much he clutched his sides in pain.

"You'll be dead before the nightfall. What do you know about survival Mars style?"

"Why don't you come and help me?"

"Ah, cutting to the chase are we now? Like I said, you're a user. You need my help and suddenly you're my friend again."

Zeke couldn't take any more. He threw back the chair and jumped to his feet.

"I AM your friend. And I thought you were mine. Seems I was mistaken."

Scuff's laughter died. Zeke turned and stormed away. But he didn't get far. A sudden pinching in his ear lifted him onto tiptoes. Despite his struggles an unseen force dragged him deep into the towering bookshelves. Trixie Cutter was waiting.

"Afternoon Earthworm," she began, her pretty face twisted into a wolfish leer.

"Let me go you psycho—!"

The stinging intensified, almost lifting Zeke off the ground.

Trixie's eyes weren't even glowing. The harder the psychics used their mind powers the more their brains heated up. This caused the small sparks of electricity that crackled through their retinal blood vessels. But Trixie's beautiful, merciless eyes had no light. For her this act of psychokinetic bullying was routine.

"You're a persistent creepy-crawly, aren't you, bluey?"

Zeke was hurting too much to answer.

"Well, let me spell things out for you. Number one, you will not speak with Barnum again. He's under my protection now. Number two, no more accusations about Professor Magma. Shut it! Otherwise things could get nasty."

"Wh-what do you mean?"

"Let's just say I'll keep your secret if you keep ours. We wouldn't want the Principal to discover you're a fake now, would we? First Go-Ship back to Earth that would be. You'll never track down your father then!"

She knew his secret!

Trixie released her psychic grip. Zeke fell to the floor.

"What about Pin-mei and Jimmy Swallow? What's happened to them?

Trixie simply winked and faded into the shadows.

Zeke stood up. She knew! And only one person could have told her—Scuff Barnum!

Zeke disliked the uncanny quiet of the Martian dawn. On Earth there would be the comfort of birdsong and traffic. He crept through the parking lot examining the Glow-Worm scooters. After a moment of indecision he chose the newest, smartest looking vehicle. Thankfully there was little security. Few students would dare steal a teacher's means of transport. With a screwdriver he undid the lid to the hard drive, replacing its chip with Albie. He threw on the switch.

The scooter purred. Its console flickered into life.

"All systems operational, Master Zeke."

"You're a solar scooter now, Albie, not a mountain bike."

"Confirmed, Sir. The upgrade is operational."

"Cool. Then we're off. The Noctis Labrynthis. Do you have the coordinates?"

"Yes, Sir. Optimal route already programmed."

Zeke sighed with relief. That was the best thing about robots, they never argued back.

"Open the storage compartment please."

A hatch at the rear popped open. Zeke stuffed his backpack inside.

"Just a few essentials until we reach Yuri-Gagarin Freetown. Nosh and dosh mostly."

Albie's only answer was the hum of his processors.

"Okay let's go. I'm, um, a bit new to motor scooters. Put rider assistance to the max."

"Understood, Sir. Suggest low speed for the first ten miles."

"Well, okay, but we need to hurry. We've a long way to go!"

Zeke swung over the saddle, and walked the vehicle back out of the bay.

"Ignition on."

The solar batteries coughed into life. Shakily Zeke steered towards the School's stone gates. As he crossed an infrared sensor they rumbled open. Mariners Valley lay beyond. A hint of daylight clung to the eastern peaks, while the canyon floor lay steeped in thick mist. Outcrops of rock loomed from the haze like ghosts. Zeke thought for a moment of his father. He felt he was somehow letting him down. Then he remembered Pin-mei's innocent smile. Without a single backward glance he stepped on the accelerator and drove out into the alien sunrise.

Chapter Twenty

Candor Chasma

Things were not going well. After twelve hours on the scooter he'd covered less than two hundred miles. A steep-sided gorge had taken him from Ophir Chasma into Candor Chasma. But the Freetown was still miles away.

He had seriously underestimated how fast the Glow-Worm could go. Although there were no roads on Mars, Zeke had assumed the major routes would be smooth after decades of use. He discovered otherwise. The dirt tracks were littered with rocks.

The sun was dropping fast. Inky shadows were creeping out from the canyon walls. There was no way to reach the settlement before nightfall. Zeke slowed to a halt.

"Albie. Plot coordinates to Melas Chasma."

"This route will reach Melas Chasma via Gagarin Freetown."

"Yes, but let's cut the Freetown and take a shortcut through the ravines. There's a Japanese outpost in Melas. Hoku...?"

"Hokusai Station. We can make it in ten hours."

Zeke's heart sank. Ten hours before civilisation! And that was without any breaks. He was exhausted and saddle sore. But there was nothing for it. Take the shortcut, camp beneath the Martian skies, and arrive at Hokusai station in the morning.

"Albie, you know, this is a fantastic adventure."

"Voice analysis indicates ninety-five percent insincerity."

"Albie."

"Yes, Master Zeke?"

"Shut up."

Zeke had left the wide-open valley and was chugging through a gully. The Glow-Worm's headlamp threw its pitiful light into the darkness. Weirdly shaped boulders emerged into its beam, one after the other, only to fade back again. Zeke was too busy fighting his ravenous hunger to feel spooked.

Albie stopped abruptly.

"Hey! Start the engine!" Zeke was furious.

"Radar indicates uncertain terrain. Recommend retreat."

"We will not! Full speed ahead."

"As you wish, Master Zeke."

The power returned but instead of movement the scooter groaned horribly. The back wheel was stuck, splattering mud in all directions.

"What the—?"

Zeke pressed firmly on the accelerator. The wheel groaned more loudly. They were trapped. The front wheel was sinking. A horrifying word leapt into Zeke's mind.

Quicksand!

The terra-forming of Mars was not without its drawbacks. One of those was the melting of immense ice deposits buried in the soil. Freezing waters seeped to the surface, causing flash floods and deadly bogs. Few survived these phenomena.

The ground around Zeke was rapidly turning to mush. Reacting instinctively he jumped off the Glow-Worm. That was a big mistake. The freezing mud sucked in his feet.

"NO!" he cried. "Albie help!"

Albie's wheels were already engulfed.

"No solution available, Master Zeke."

"I'LL DIE! THERE MUST BE SOMETHING!"

"Recommend closedown and await rescue."

The computerised Glow-Worm clicked and its lights faded. That was the worst thing about robots. They didn't worry about dying.

Zeke was up to his knees. He tried to pull his right leg out. Nothing.

"HELP!"

The word bounced off faraway cliffs and echoed back. It was useless. He hadn't seen a soul all day. With every ounce of strength he strained against the bog. This just made him drop faster.

The Glow-Worm tipped forward, rapidly submerging. The handlebars sunk first, then the saddle. Finally, with a sickening *slurp* the taillight disappeared. Albie and the scooter were gone.

"HELP ME! SOMEBODY PLEASE!" he screamed.

Surely it wasn't going to end like this, so unexpectedly, so pointlessly? There had to be a way out.

The icy quicksand tightened its grip. His thighs were vanishing. Zeke was all out of options.

"GRAB THE LINE!"

Hope surged through Zeke's heart. Rescue! And that accent was familiar. The headlamp of another Glow-Worm was shining twenty yards back down the gully. A tow cable shot through the night air. It landed short!

"Damn!" cursed the rescuer, silhouetted by his lights. He flicked a switch and the cable retracted into the wheel guard. He fired again.

"YES!" Zeke cried.

This time it fell within reach. But as Zeke leaned over he lost balance and toppled. Splash! The bitter-cold slush dragged him under. For a moment everything was chaos. He resurfaced, on his stomach and moving. Somehow he had caught the cable and was hanging on with every ounce of strength.

The ground beneath his torso hardened as he left the quicksand behind. Zeke let go of the cable and lay exhausted, heaving and gasping like a beached fish. His clothes were saturated with icy mud. His limbs were trembling. He felt as cold and wet as an iceberg.

The newcomer towered over him, a dark figure against the glittering night sky. Zeke drew a deep breath, stilled his shaky legs, and staggered to his feet.

"Decided to come to your senses then?" he said, as coolly as he could manage.

"You Brits and your stiff upper lips!" Scuff laughed and squashed him in a bear hug.

The happy reunion was short-lived. Zeke saw the horror spreading across Scuff's face. The ground was turning squishy beneath their shoes.

"Zeke! On the count of three jump."

"Jump!?"

"Onto this boulder." Scuff nodded to the wall of rock beside them.

Zeke glanced up. Had his friend gone crazy? It was too steep and too high.

"Just jump and imagine there's no gravity. Visualise flying the last few feet to the top." Scuff took Zeke's hands in his.

"B-b-but—"

"JUST DO IT!"

Their feet were disappearing into the mire.

"One, two, three, JUMP!"

They leapt high in the weak gravity, but lost momentum and began to fall. Then an unseen force grabbed them and heaved them the higher.

Chapter Twenty-One

Between a rock and a soft place

They sat on the summit for a long time without speaking. Zeke rested his chin on his knees, shivering. Scuff sprawled on his back. His rescue beacon bleeped monotonously behind him.

"So that's why it's called the Milky Way," he remarked.

The night was saturated with starlight.

"It's just so—"

"Milky?" Zeke suggested.

"Totally, bro. Awesome! To think Martians once looked at these same stars, all those millions of years ago."

"Well, they were different then. The constellations."

"You're joking?"

"I never joke about astronomy. I'm a fully paid-up member of the London Galactarium."

"That's the antique space museum? Three hundred years old or something?"

"Right, but it's still fantastic. I learnt so much from their shows on the night sky. Stars travel at mind-boggling speeds. But across distances so, um, mind-bogglingly big we can't see the difference. Not even in a thousand years. But the Hesperians lived two billion years ago. The stars made different patterns back then."

"How come you're so crazy for astronomy, anyway?"

Zeke glanced down.

"My father, I suppose. When I was little I would look out my bedroom window every night. Always hoping for a sign of my dad."

"What? A message written in star beams?"

Zeke made an effort to stop his chattering teeth.

"Silly isn't it. But I was only a little kid."

Scuff stared at the ground too. "When I was a tiny tot I thought my dad was the Prime Minister of Canada. Not the president of a company selling second-rate fusion reactors."

A pause settled in the frosty air.

"The temps really plummet after dark, don't they?" Scuff went on. "There was a foil blanket in my Glow-Worm."

"I could really do with that. Pity it's halfway to the planet's core."

"You should worry. I have to tell Mariner Flounder I lost his beloved scooter. I'm going to have to fork out some serious compensation!"

"You should have stolen one. A lot less complicated."

Scuff threw a pebble over the ledge. The sound of a splash confirmed their fears. Zeke attempted a smile.

"So we're trapped. I wonder what's going to kill me first? The cold or your jokes?"

"Seriously, bro, sooner or later Mars Valley Rescue will pick up our signal."

"They better get here before I freeze solid. That quicksand was arctic! Anyway, why were you hanging out with Trixie Cutter's gang?"

Scuff chuckled. "They were hanging out with me, actually."

"But why?"

"Well it doesn't take a telepath to read Snod's mind. Obviously he was keeping an eye on me. Making sure I didn't help you."

"What reason would they have for that?"

"You tell me."

Zeke, despite his tiredness, recounted everything that had happened since they broke into Lutz's office, the engraving, the Spiral, the Dust Devil, Lieutenant Doughty, the Orb of Can-do, and the Infinity Trap.

"Wow!" was all that Scuff could say.

Zeke suddenly lowered his gaze and stared at the ground. A silence as immense as the great sky above weighed down upon them.

"Bro? What is it?" Scuff asked at last.

Zeke lifted his head. His eyes, full of hurt, met Scuff's.

"Why did you tell them?"

"Sorry?"

"You told Trixie my secret. Why?"

"Sheesh! She knows?"

"Don't pretend you didn't tell her."

Scuff scratched his ear.

"Bro, honestly. But you know, she insisted I meet Alonzo Caracol."

"El telepático?"

"Right, Mexico's greatest junior telepathist. I thought he was staring at me oddly. Must have been sifting through my brain for info."

Zeke fell quiet again, thinking it all through.

"Okay, forgiven."

He began shivering more violently.

"Hey, bro, want my jacket? Before your teeth fall out?"

"Not especially, I'm feeling warmer."

Scuff gave his friend an odd look.

"Warmer?" He slipped off his thermal coat and handed it over. Zeke accepted it with a grunt.

"You know, bro, you made me so mad dumping me in the Principal's office. Guess I needed time to glue my ego back in one piece."

"Yes, sorry about that."

"Okey-dokey. Maybe we both got carried away."

Scuff gave a gawky smile. Zeke returned it with his own lopsided grin.

"So, wanna hear about your dad?"

Zeke forced open his droopy eyes. "Tell away!"

"He graduated with Distinction. Special commendation from Lutz as an outstanding student."

"Where did he go? What was his mission?"

"The only mention was that years later he joined the Flying Dutchman Project. But what that was, or where he went, well, not a nano-byte."

"It's a good start. Scuff, you're the best friend I've ever had." Zeke's voice was sluggish and slurred.

"Scuff, do you think you can love someone you've never met?"

"Your dad? That's natcho, it's a father and son thing."

"I feel like I've failed him, putting him on the backburner while I track down Pin."

"Zeke, he'll be fine with it. Totally."

Strangely Zeke's limbs stopped shivering. Scuff jabbed him in the ribs.

"OW!"

"Keep talking, bro."

"About what?"

"Um, spot quiz. What's the population of Mars?"

"Who cares?" Zeke replied, struggling to stay awake.

"Over a million."

Zeke giggled. "Where are they all when we need them?"

"The Big Pumpkin's hardly an asteroid. One million is a drop in the ocean. Your turn."

There was an urgency in Scuff's voice. He poked Zeke again. "*Your turn.*"

Zeke sat bolt upright. "Ocean? Yes! You're swimming in the dead ocean!"

Scuff didn't reply. He knew it was the hypothermia talking.

Zeke slumped onto his side, unconscious. His body was giving up.

Chapter Twenty-Two

The Medical Facility

For a long, dreamy time Zeke gazed at the surface of Mars. He remembered his first sighting, ninety miles high in Edward Dayo's Go-Ship. Somehow the surface was different this time. As his eyes slowly focused, he realised it was near enough to touch. Zeke was looking at the roof of a cave.

He lifted his head.

"Ouch!" His neck ached. In fact every muscle in his body ached. "Is it flu?" he asked no one in particular.

"Hardly," laughed a voice.

Zeke blinked and took in his surroundings. He was in the Medical Facility. A young, beautiful woman in a white coat sat at her computer typing notes. It was the school medic, Dr Chandrasar.

"Take it easy, Mr Hailey. You've been out for three days."

"What!" Zeke cried, and sat up.

"Hypothermia. A falling of the body temperature below that necessary for normal metabolism."

Zeke stared at her blankly.

"To be expected after skinny-dipping in ice water."

"I wasn't skinny-dipping."

The doctor turned towards him with a radiant smile on her catlike face. "Forgive me, I didn't mean to make light of your predicament. It's a remarkable story. Barnum is quite the school hero."

"Scuff?"

"He used psychokinesis to warm the air around your body. I understand the emergency rotorcopter took ages to reach you. All that time Scuff kept you alive with an air blanket. Ingenious really. If only I were psychic, I'd use those powers to save lives, not go gallivanting around the galaxy."

The doctor was one of the few people at the Chasm who was not extrasensory. Zeke dearly yearned to tell her he was another.

"Scuff's been awarded the Ophir Chasma Cross."

Zeke knew he should be grateful but deep down he felt jealous. A school full of special kids, at times he wanted to throw up. Chandrasar saw his expression.

"You did well, too. Scuff told us how your powers lifted you both out of the quicksand, up onto that boulder."

"Oh, yes, that's right, Doctor." It was good of Scuff to cover for him but Zeke still felt an idiot among eggheads.

"I've been here for three days?"

"Yes, Mars Valley Rescue airlifted you here. I've had you sedated while the nanotherapy did its work. But you're fully recovered. I imagine you can sleep in your room tonight."

A gleam of fear darted through Chandrasar's dark brown eyes.

"As long as you lock your door."

"Whatever for?"

"Hans Kretzmer, Year Three. Vanished in the night! Lutz has instigated a curfew. Good thing for her all your parents are on another planet. On Earth the whole school would be closed. On Mars, of course, one can get away with murder, not to mention kidnapping."

L ate in the afternoon Scuff popped his chubby face around the door.

"Howdy, bro, how's tricks."

"The Doc said I could go home today, if the assessments are okay. She's just gone to the lab to pick them up."

"Okey-dokey. Guess you heard about Hans Knees and Bumpsy-daisy. I remembered what you said and went to investigate his room. Just like you said, bro, a dust trail all the way to the busted exit."

"The same creature that got Pin, who, incidentally, we are no nearer saving."

"Chill out, bro. You'll do it. Now, remember levitating us the last few feet to the top of that damn rock?"

"There you go again. Messing with my head."

Scuff sat down on the bedside.

"Listen up, Zeke. We flew the last five feet of that jump by mind power alone. And I didn't do it, deliberately."

Zeke glared at his friend coldly.

"Lets face it," Scuff went on. "Left to me and we would've crash landed back in the dippy doo!"

"Rather brave of you, wasn't it? Staking our lives on the slim chance I might have some psychic gift in here." Zeke tapped his skull angrily.

"You forget I'm a genius. I figure it's a survival thing. Faced with danger your subconscious springs into action."

"So how long have you been studying Fantasy 101?"

Scuff was lost for a reply. At that moment Chandrasar breezed into the Medical Facility with Zeke's results.

"Not a chill bone in your body. You're free to go."

Scuff said, "Doc. Do you have anyway of testing for psychic powers?"

"Not here. That's what the ESP exam is for. We'd need a psychometer. Why?"

Scuff took a deep gulp. "My friend here, well, he's having doubts."

"Shut up!" Zeke growled. The nerd was giving the game away!

Chandrasar pulled up a chair. She took Zeke's hand in hers.

"That's very common. Every year I have newbies in here telling me there's been a terrible mistake. They've been sent to the wrong school. The exams papers got mixed up, etcetera, etcetera. And I give them my professional diagnosis. They have a case of the cold feet, or homesickness, or just a plain old blue funk. But whatever their symptoms the treatment's the same."

"Which is?" Zeke asked.

"Believe in yourself."

"Believe in myself? What? Believe I can fly and I will?"

"Principal Lutz flies everyday."

"BUT I'M NOT PSYCHIC!" Zeke didn't mean to shout, the words just came out that way.

"Keep saying that long enough and it will come true. But why don't you try some positive thinking? Faith can move mountains, and I'm not talking psychokinesis."

Their eyes met. Zeke could see she was sincere. And Chandrasar was a doctor after all, no fool.

Scuff cleared his throat. "That's all our gifts are, anyway, Zeke. Faith. Whether it's bending spoons or seeing the future. It's all in the mind."

"Why isn't everybody psychic then? Why isn't Dr. Chandrasar a Mariner? Either you've got the gift or not."

The doctor smiled sweetly. "Well maybe I could if I wanted it hard enough. Science tells us all humans are born wired for extrasensory ability. Why only a tiny percentage go ahead to become full-blown psychics isn't known yet."

Zeke wanted to speak but the words died on his lips.

Chandrasar continued, "You know I did have a dream that came true once. That's what brought me to Mars. People aren't totally psychic or totally not. Everyone has potential. Imagine a line, a few people are at the low end, most are in the middle but a special few come right at the top. Those are the ones chosen to become Mariners."

Nobody spoke.

Chandrasar stood up. "Well, you're free to go, Zeke. Let me just get your clothes from the laundry. I can't have you turning up to class in jim-jams."

Both boys laughed. The doctor left the room.

"Tell me again how you faked your exam results?" Scuff asked.

Zeke sighed. Earth and his old school seemed light years ago.

"There was a psychic in my class. Felix Dyer—"

"How did you know he was one of us?"

"Um, he was forever doing tricks. You know, card tricks, think-of-a-number tricks—"

"Sounds more like a conjuring act."

"A week before the exams I found him in the loos sobbing his heart out. Turns out he had vertigo and was terrified of going up the Televator. Never mind translocating to Mars."

"And?"

"And I spotted my opportunity. To track down Dad."

"Yes I know all about your heroic daddy. Tell me about this Felix."

"We came up with a system. Foot tapping and coughs. A code for exchanging our pass numbers in the exams."

"The sealed numbers given out with the exam papers?"

"Exactly. At the end of the exam he typed my number into his computer and I did his."

"So in effect you swapped your exam answers."

"Clever huh?"

Scuff stroked his chin.

"Seems kosher enough. Maybe you're just a late developer. Hey, I'm late myself! Time to give Flounder another nervous breakdown."

"Thanks, by the way, for saving my life."

Scuff grinned from the doorway.

"No sweat, Zeke. That's what buddies are for."

As he left Chandrasar returned with Zeke's clothes. Despite a long soak in the laundromac, Zeke could still smell the Martian bog on them.

"If I hurry I can make Psychokinesis 101."

Chandrasar smiled. "Ah, about that. Orders from Lutz. Straight to her office for detention."

"Detention!"

"You steal a Mariner's Glow-Worm and nearly get yourselves killed? I'd think myself lucky if I were you."

"But detention. Can't you tell her I'm still sick?"

"Violate my Hippocratic oath? Thou shall not fib to the School Principal? Never! She's planning an evening of great poems from the English language."

"Poetry! That's inhuman. Not poetry!"

"The last student caught stealing was handed over to the authorities. Lutz obviously likes you. Now scat!"

Zeke had one last question. "What was your dream? The one that came true?"

"That, young friend, is a long story," Chandrasar said, and with moist eyes showed him to the door.

Chapter Twenty-Three

The School Secretary's Office

Zeke felt as if his eyes were about to pop. He sneaked a glimpse of his watch. Only nine o'clock!

"Miss, can I finish? My wrist is killing me."

The school secretary glared at him with all the compassion of a hangman. "Principal Lutz was quite specific. Ten copies of the Rime of the Ancient Mariner. You, I see, have only done eight."

Zeke sighed. His fingers were throbbing. But he knew it was useless to beg for mercy. Marjorie Barnside had a heart of steel. Every student in the Chasm said so.

"Where are you up to?"

Zeke skimmed down the electrobook.

"Um, 'Like one that on a lonesome road, doth walk in fear and dread—'"

"Ah yes," the secretary said, interrupting. "And having once turned round walks on, and turns no more his head; because he knows a frightful fiend doth close behind him tread."

Zeke raised his eyebrows.

"Ach, I have a photographic memory. And it's the Principal's favourite for detentions. Over the years an awful lot of bad boys and girls have passed through this institution."

Zeke looked at the silver frame on her desk with its hundred year old photo. "How long have you worked here, Miss?"

"None of your business, young man. Now back to your efforts, please."

Zeke bowed his head and resumed copy writing. A few minutes elapsed.

"Ach, are you making that noise?" the secretary asked suddenly, pushing her seat away from the computer. Zeke stared at her vacantly.

"Listen," she said, sweeping an iron-grey lock of hair back into place.

At first there was nothing. Then Zeke heard it too! A whooshing sound, distant but coming closer. A lump of fear clogged up his throat.

"Miss, lock the door and call for help!"

Barnside stood up.

"Don't be a wee bairn. Concentrate on your lines."

The stocky woman stomped over to the open door. She peered down the gloomy staircase.

"Nobody? Yet I hear something. Curious."

Zeke leapt to his feet. Panic was bubbling through his ribcage. He knew exactly what was approaching. "Lock the door!"

The office photon lamps flickered and died. Zeke grabbed the magnophone from the desk. It was dead.

"My goodness, what in the devil's name goes there?"

"COME AWAY FROM THE DOOR!"

Zeke cast an eye over the secretary's broad shoulders. The Dust Devil was marching up around the steps, a spinning cloud of sand with the luminous figure at its core.

To Zeke's despair the secretary remained resolutely in the doorway. The whirlwind reached the top, silhouetting Barnside's hefty figure in its glow. She raised her hand in defiance.

"Whatever you are I deny you access. This student is my responsibility and I am authorized by the office of the Ophir Chasma School to use force in his protection."

The creature made a noise like laughter.

It walked towards the doorway and embraced her in its swirling chaos. For a moment nothing happened. Then, slowly, the stony-faced Barnside lifted off the ground and began rotating. Zeke watched helplessly as she gathered speed. Then the Dust Devil released her. The secretary flew through the air and crashed into the wall, collapsing in a shower of sparks. A jumble of wires burst from her ruptured shoulder. Her limbs jerked in spasms and her lips twitched. Then, with a puff of smoke, her body came to a complete stop.

"You're an android?" Zeke gasped.

There was no time to take it in. The Dust Devil was moving into the room.

ESCAPE! screamed Zeke's inner voice. But how? The window was a sheer drop of a hundred and fifty feet. The only other door led to Lutz's office but that was locked.

The head of the Dust Devil swivelled on its shifting neck. Although it had no eyes it was clearly searching for him. Perhaps, Zeke thought, it sees in another way. In any case it had found him. The monster glided nearer, two yards with every pace.

The terror was too much.

"GET ME OUT OF HERE!"

For a split second he seemed to be at the bottom of a deep sea. *Then, inexplicably, he was outside the office, on the landing!* Wasting no time, Zeke hurtled down the stairs, three at a time.

"Don't slip. Don't slip," he cried through clenched teeth.

Never had a stairwell seemed so endless. His shadow ran before him, cast by the light of the demon at his heels. Zeke tripped at the last step, landing in a heap. Instantly he picked himself up and tore down the corridor. Thanks to Lutz's curfew it was deserted. Had she set the whole thing up? Trap Zeke at the top of her tower and make sure there were no witnesses?

He glanced back. The Dust Devil was advancing, incredibly fast despite its leisurely strides. Zeke's mind raced, but there were no answers. He hadn't a hope of outrunning it.

Zeke rushed past a couple of cleanomacs, plugged into the wall circuits and recharging. The robots couldn't help him, but supposing—?

Zeke skidded to a halt. Grabbing hold of the closest mac he flipped its manual control button. The powerful engine in its belly groaned into life as the Dust Devil closed in. Desperately Zeke yanked the suction tube out from the robot's brush-feet.

"Abduct this!" he shouted, aiming the suction tube at the Dust Devil. The creature shrieked. The tube began sucking in its powdery body. Zeke was winning. But then the creature pulled back. With a violent jolt the machine wrenched free of Zeke's grip. The Dust Devil effortlessly lifted the cleanomac and hurled it away, smashing it to pieces.

"Oh-oh."

Zeke pivoted on one foot, about to run. Too late! The Dust Devil grabbed him by the hand. Cold, stinging sand blasted Zeke's skin. His foothold gave way and he tumbled onto the polished stone. Frantically he scrambled back from the monster, staring up at its empty face.

"STOP!" he hollered with all his strength.

The monster ignored him, reaching down again.

THINK! Screamed the voice in Zeke's head.

"*Mnthax!*"

The Dust Devil froze.

"*Mnthax!*" Zeke said again, just to be sure. The creature understood Hesperian! The word meant stop. But what now? Fired by adrenalin, Zeke dredged the vocabulary he needed from his subconscious.

"*Who are you?*" he said in the alien tongue.

The Dust Devil stirred. A slit of a mouth opened and a tongue of dry sand coughed out primeval syllables.

"*New Master calls me Caliban.*"

138

The new Master? That had to be Magma.

"What's your real name?"

It didn't answer.

"What are you?"

"Something forgotten."

Zeke's mind flashed back to the Orb of Can-do and the Hesperian text Magma was so determined to translate.

"What is the Infinity Trap?"

The living twister groaned.

"A secret."

It jerked its head to one side.

"You are maker. Cannot take maker. Must find other."

"No-o-o!"

The monster slid past him towards the dormitories and quickly disappeared.

Briefly, Zeke lay panting like racehorse. He pulled himself together and ran through the corridor, bawling one word as loud as he could. "INTRUDER!!!"

Chapter Twenty-Four

Scuff's Room Again

Henrietta Lutz's face emerged from the computer screen, as if she were about to climb through. But it was merely the holographic bulletin. The lips began moving.

"It is with heavy heart that my office must announce the disappearance of another student, fourth year Yong-Ho Moon. He is an exemplary young man with an academic record many of you might wish to aspire to. I want to reassure the School that everything is being done to end this crime spree.

"I have spoken to the Governor of Mars who promised to send a security detail immediately. In the meantime I must extend the curfew indefinitely. All students are to be locked in their rooms by seven PM. Please activate your intruder alarms. I suggest you put this time to good use by revising for the end of term exams.

"As is often the way in times of great concern, a false rumour is circulating the corridors. Let me make it clear that my long-serving secretary, Marjorie Barnside was not injured in last night's incident. Indeed she is here with me now as steadfast and industrious as ever. Anyone claiming otherwise is a victim of mass hysteria and will be detained for treatment."

The face faded.

"Wow oh wow oh wow." Scuff said, sitting on his bed. "Wow, oh wow, oh wowee!" he sang, totally off key.

"Put a sock in it," Zeke snapped.

Scuff continued caterwauling. Zeke picked up two of Scuff's stinky socks from the floor. He rolled them into a ball and lobbed them at his friend.

"Typical of you. Always so literal." Scuff smirked.

"It's no laughing matter."

"No it ain't, bro. You're probably the first ever human to talk with an alien. You discovered batty Barnside is an illegal android. You're totally fluent in Martian and can translocate. It's a most exciting matter, that's what it is."

"Are you sure Barnside is illegal? Mars is outside Earth's authority, after all."

"Dunno. But she's certainly hot contraband on Earth. All fake humans were outlawed ninety years ago, following the Dummy Presidents Plot."

"Oh, we did that in History. Some loony was replacing the world's top leaders with android copies."

"Yep. The worst thing was the androids made a better job of world peace than the real life presidents."

"Maybe that's what's happening here? The real Lutz has been replaced with an android. That's why she's working for Magma."

Scuff leant forward.

"No way, bro. I've seen that woman translocate and levitate. No such thing as a psychic robot, remember. Anyway, it's your dust devil creature that's the biggie here."

Zeke chewed on his pen. "He was pretty amazing. Wish I'd had more time with him. He must know where Pin is!" He flushed and snapped his pen in two. "WE'RE DOING NOTHING TO SAVE HER!"

"Keep cool, bro. You're right. And the School doesn't seem to be lifting an extrasensory finger, nor his highness the Governor of the Big Red Zero."

"It's up to us."

"It's up to us. But Noctis Labyrinthis is way too far to reach by mountain bike or solar scooter. We need serious transport, something hardcore. I'm working on it, bro. Just trust me for now."

"Why don't we ask the older students to translocate us there."

"I've tried. No one would do it. Translocation takes years of practice to cross vast distances safely. Sidestepping reality from inside to outside an office is one thing. Leaping a thousand miles is quite another."

"Do you really think I translocated?"

"Totally. One second you're inside then the next you're outside. That was your subconscious responding to a life-threatening situation."

Zeke clenched the broken pen between his teeth. "It's not the first time. The day Pin-mei was abducted. I was running to the bike stands. All I could think about was how desperately I needed to get there. Then suddenly I was. But why doesn't it work when I try. I've been practising for hours."

"Okay, let's have a go. Put that sad, sorry pen you're abusing on the desktop."

Zeke obeyed. Scuff fixed him with a confident stare.

"Breath deeply. That's good. Empty your mind. That shouldn't be too tricky for you. Focus on the pen. Visualise it rising, ever so gently. Just a few millimetres for starters. Lift it with your mind. Focus, that's it, focus. Harder."

Nothing.

"*Bthphrx!*" Zeke cursed and flicked the pen halfway across the room.

"I won't ask what that means," Scuff said, aiming the remote at his computer. It whirred into life. "I've spent hours trawling the Mars-Wide-Web, The Encyclopaedia Marius, even the School's electro–library. And not a clue about Spirals, sentient whirlwinds, or orbs. The only information I could access was the school test results. Look at this."

Scuff opened a holo-cube and brought up rows and rows of figures.

"What on Mars has that got to do with anything?"

"These are the end-of-term psychic exam scores."

"So?"

"I put every total from last year into one chart. Now, look at the top ten students."

Zeke wolf-whistled.

"Three of the kidnapped students are on the list."

"Right, bro, the only name missing is Pin-mei, who hasn't done any exams yet. But she's an outstanding precog, and knew something about Magma's plot."

Zeke whistled again.

"Look here, Trixie Cutter and her sidekick Alonzo are also top tenners."

"Right," Scuff replied. "And no doubt Magma offered them protection in return for working for him."

"What is it she does for him?"

"Information gathering. I heard her say that."

"Spying more like. And she set up Pin-mei's abduction." Zeke's brow creased. "I was just thinking, Magma asked me to translate that Hesperian for him. 'The key is a brain'. Maybe that's why he's kidnapping the best psychics. Something to do with the Infinity Trap."

"Maybe, bro. But what is an Infinity Trap? What does it do?"

"It's connected to the Spiral. I just know it."

"Which is what exactly? A machine, an alien?"

Zeke banged the desk with his fist. "I don't know but there's one place we can find out."

Zeke peeked through the circular window of the boy's toilets and across to the stairwell leading to Lutz's pinnacle. He glanced again at his wristwatch. It was eight o'clock, one hour into the curfew. The outer corridor was as pitch black as inside the toilets.

"Oh!" he gasped. The beam of a torch sliced through the darkness. He crept quickly back to one of the cubicles, sat down on the loo, and closed the door. If the torch belonged to Drufus Slatts he was safe. But it might be one of the Mariners. Lutz had hastily organised a night-shift patrol.

The main door creaked on its hinges. Zeke sucked in his breath. Who was it? The rendezvous with the senior student wasn't till eight-thirty.

Drufus Slatts was a huge plank of a boy, not particularly bright but a solid translocator. He was however extremely broke, after using the weekend trips permitted to older students to lose a fortune at the Freetown casinos. Scuff promised him a handsome reward if he translocated Zeke into Lutz's office. Neither Zeke nor Scuff had any further appetite for cockroach pills.

Footsteps padded towards Zeke's cubicle. The light darted around the ceiling. Then came a knock.

"Drufus, is that you?" Zeke hissed.

Again somebody's knuckles rapped on the door. Biting his thumb Zeke pulled back the door. A tall shadow before him aimed the torch back on its face.

It was Mariner Knimble, gloating from ear to ear.

Chapter Twenty-Five

An unexpected encounter

"**D**rufus Slatts will not be keeping his appointment." Knimble grinned.

"So he's a sneak as well as a moron."

"Tsk, tsk. Such harsh words. Actually Drufus didn't tell. He's in my Translocation class. As soon as he walked through the door I knew something was up. His skull should be made of glass, it's so see-through."

"You read his mind? Isn't that bad manners?"

Knimble stroked his goatee. "Normally yes, but in times of crisis the Mariners must do everything in their power to protect the Earthworms."

Zeke hung his head in dismay.

"In any case it's difficult not to with Drufus. Quite unlike—"

Zeke glanced up. Knimble was staring at him with that faraway expression. Zeke suddenly felt as though his mind were a book and the Mariner was leafing through its pages.

"Quite unlike other more unfathomable students. That's an excellent thought-shield for a newbie. Have you been practicing?"

Zeke went to reply but bit his tongue.

"You didn't know you were deflecting? Strewth. Must be instinct."

Knimble leaned nearer. His eyes began to radiate softly. "I could break down that wall if I wished. Discover just what secrets you are so keen to conceal."

He pulled back sharply. His eye sockets dulled. "Still, you're entitled to your privacy. Where were we?"

"Detention and a one-way ticket back to Earth, I expect," Zeke said with a scowl.

"Aha! Never make assumptions. Slatts' deafening brainwaves told me you're planning another trip to the principal's office. Is it about that revolting Martian fossil?"

Zeke nodded.

"I see. And you need to translocate there, avoiding all the surveillance cams and security locks."

Zeke nodded again.

"Well then, kiddo, why don't you let me take you there. I'm the best translocator in the building."

Zeke's jaw dropped.

Knimble chuckled. "Your thoughts tell me you believe you're telling the truth. With students disappearing we've got to investigate any clue, however farfetched it sounds."

"Why won't Lutz take my word, when you will?"

Knimble shrugged. "She's been principal for a very long time. The idea she might be wrong about anything is beyond her."

Or she's in on the whole affair! Zeke thought.

"Isn't it a bit risky? Helping the school bad boy?" he said.

"I wasn't always a boring old Mariner. Did you know that as a boy I got expelled from the Chasm?"

"N-no."

"Sure, mate. But keep it under your hat. Anyway, your father was a decent sort, and something tells me you are too."

Zeke smiled. Knimble was okay for a teacher.

The Mariner straightened his back. "As I said, we've got to do everything in our power to save the students. Just swear you'll never tell it was me."

"Cross my heart."

"Excellent. Now put your hands on my shoulders. That's it."

Zeke stepped closer. Knimble's white uniform reeked of curry.

"Here we go."

Emptiness yawned beneath their feet. Zeke's stomach churned.

"Let go, Hailey."

They were standing in Lutz's office. The towering filing cabinets were lit by a silvery light.

"Phobos is overhead. How convenient," Knimble said, craning his neck to the skylights.

"When we translocated from Earth to Mars, it was—"

"A more profound experience? Mass fainting, hysteria, etcetera?"

"Yep," Zeke said.

"Well Earth to Mars is a very long distance. Downstairs to upstairs isn't."

"But then Mars is just down the street in comparison to Deep Space. I just can't believe people travel that far by thinking."

"Deep Space travel has assistance. Farships are fitted with biological amplifiers. You'll learn about that when you're older."

Zeke thought for a moment. "Why are you helping me do this, Sir? Really?"

"Oh, just keeping my inner rebel alive."

"What was it you did? To get expelled?"

"I hung a pair of knickers from the top of this very minaret."

"Really! And they expelled you for that?"

"Master Hailey, can't you guess whose knickers they were?"

"Gosh, you don't mean?"

Knimble tapped his nose with his forefinger. "Some secrets are best left buried. Not to mention some people's underwear."

They both laughed. The Mariner aimed his torch at the engraving behind the desk.

"Lets see this Martian magic, then," he said.

Zeke approached the picture. The runes were waiting to be read.

"Dthoth thla ryksi thngai bchrfft xgiishi dthoth thla gleqxuus jchzaa."

The rectangle of stone remained unchanged. It wasn't working. Then the torchlight faltered. Zeke turned back to Knimble. The man was perfectly still.

"Mariner Knimble?"

Something was wrong but in the darkness it was hard to see. Zeke reached out a finger. The teacher's uniform disintegrated beneath his touch. It was sand!

"AHH!" Zeke shrieked, whipping his hand away. It was too late. The figure of his teacher crumbled before his eyes.

Zeke gasped, stepping backwards. And then another step. And then—

Zeke stopped falling. He was back inside the picture. Examining his geometrical body confirmed he was two-dimensional again. Triangles surrounded him. A row zigzagged above his head and another around his feet. They reminded Zeke of stalactites and stalagmites.

Zeke concentrated, conjuring up the Hesperian words.

"What's going on?" His voice boomed through the empty cavern.

Silence. Zeke shouted out again. Black dots appeared all around him, expanding into circles with smaller dots inside them. They were cells, multiplying, dividing and sub-dividing. It was like drowning in frogspawn.

"Welcome back, Earth Child. We are pleased to see you." The spawn pulsated as it spoke.

"Your command of our language is greatly improved. Well done."

A hundred questions were burning in Zeke's head. Fearful that this audience might be short lived, he pressed on. "Firstly, what are you?"

"A recording. A collection of thoughts, memories and ideas."

"Are you Hesperians?"

"As we said, we are their thoughts. Perhaps your culture does not preserve mental energy in the same way?"

"I'm confused. You make yourself sound like a computer. But you're alive."

"Are those things contradictory?"

Zeke decided not to get bogged down in the details. "So you contain data on the Hesperian race?"

"Less and less. Our memory atoms are corroding."

"What?"

"Our makers never envisaged we would last such a very, very long time. Soon we will cease."

"Tell me about that Dust Devil thing. How did you know he was after my friend?"

"He is *dthpʒpii*, a guardian. We sense his movements."

"What does he guard?"

"The Infinity Trap."

The excitement was too much to bear. Finally Zeke was getting somewhere. "So tell me about the Infinity Trap."

"It's a shortcut."

Zeke tried to make sense of it all. "Similar to *translocation*?" He used the earth word but the cells seemed to understand.

"The Infinity Trap exists from the dawn of the Universe to its end, connecting up all times and realities."

"Wow! Like parallel dimensions?"

"Among other things."

Zeke tried to whistle through his geometric lips. It made translocation sound feeble. "What's the Spiral?"

A tremor ran through the spawn. They were frightened. "The Spiral is the darkness in the depths of our soul."

"Did it destroy the Hesperians?"

"We don't remember."

Zeke was stumped. That was not the answer he expected. "What has the Spiral got to do with the Infinity Trap?"

The cells paused. "We don't know, but it's a good way for the Spiral to return."

"Return?"

"According to Hesperian mythology, the Spiral is a cosmic demon cast out of this Universe in the violent moments of its beginning. The Spiral is outside, ravenously hungry."

"Hungry?"

"For everything living."

With a shudder Zeke recalled his previous trip inside the Engraving and the simulation of the Spiral's attack. "But the Spiral already came back. You showed me."

"We showed you fragments, not the complete story. The Hesperians knew a way to stop it, but we have lost that information."

Zeke stamped his diagrammatical foot in frustration. "So what can you tell me? What about the guardian? How can I—"

"More apologies, Earth Child. You have drained our power molecules. You must go, for your own welfare. It will be a few days before we can reactivate. And your next visit must be your last, regrettably."

"Why? Why?"

"Our strength, like our memories, is waning. We will be unable to open up to you after that."

Zeke panicked.

"WAIT! How can I overcome the guardian?"

The cells were shrinking rapidly, forming light and dark patches. They were metamorphosing into an image, like pixels. The image of a face. The face talked.

"Strewth, kidda, for a moment there I thought you were a gonner."

It was Knimble, leaning over Zeke and checking his pulse.

Chapter Twenty-Six

Scuff's dream

Scuff was swimming, fully dressed, through a warm, shallow sea. Metallic-green fish darted through the glassy waters. Cherry red clouds drifted overhead. Scuff's favourite neighbourhood restaurant, *Baron Von Burgers*, lay ahead, bobbing like a boathouse on the gentle current.

"Odd," he puffed between strokes. "Why isn't that in Lakeville where it belongs?"

Scuff heaved himself onto the floating diner and pushed through the glass doors. A six-foot beetle was serving behind the counter, dressed as a World War One fighter pilot. As Scuff queued up he realised the creature's face was more human than bug.

"It's an insectoid, like an insect but not," whispered another customer in his ear. Scuff turned to see Tiberius Magma, with a whizzing spiral where his face should be.

"Whaddaya want?" the insectoid boomed in a thick New York accent.

Scuff ordered Chicken X-treme with a side of fries and a jumbo soda. He sat by the window, opposite Trixie Cutter. She was too busy cramming burgers down her throat to notice him. Tomato ketchup smeared her face and her flowery-pink blouse.

THUMP!

The soda rippled in its plastic cup. The fries jumped on their plate.

THUMP!

This time the whole ocean trembled.

"Quit with the banging. You wanna start a tsunami?" the Insectoid bellowed.

THUMP!

A grey shadow rose on the horizon. A giant wave. The customers began screaming, only they weren't people anymore. They looked more like jellyfish, slithering around in blind panic. The room went dark.

THUMP!

"You wanna start a tsunami, bro?" a disorientated Scuff barked, waking up in his room.

A wide-eyed Zeke was banging at his door. "We've got to go NOW. Whatever transport you've been dropping hints about, is it ready?"

"Sheesh, bro, it's five in the morning, can't this wait till breakfast?"

"NO! Have you got the wheels?"

"Hah, kind of. I take it Drufus showed up. When's he collecting his reward?"

Zeke slowed down. "Actually he didn't. Mariner Knimble took me up, but swear you'll keep it secret."

Scuff's eyebrows rose as high as they could. "A Mariner broke into the principal's office? I'm shocked!"

Zeke grabbed Scuff by the upper arms. "We have to go NOW."

"What about your father? Searching the school for more clues?"

"We've got to put that aside! Magma doesn't know what he's tampering with. If I'm right we're all in danger."

"You mean the entire School?"

"I mean the entire galaxy."

Scuff's lips stuck like glue. He wished he were back at the Baron Von Burgers.

"Okay, bro, get your copy of Albie and meet me here in ten minutes."

I t was still night when the two boys crept from the Southern Entrance. The courtyard was dark and quiet. The sky was as crowded with stars as always. The school Millipede was parked across the gravel, a great, slumbering robot.

"You've hired it? Bought it?" Zeke asked.

Scuff chuckled. "Our mode of travel is parked behind."

They hurried around the silver legs.

"Oh!" Zeke cried. "A helicopter!"

A red mottled two-seater was tucked behind the Millipede. A long mast rose above the bubble of its cockpit, blades unopened. A huge fan propeller was bolted onto the rear.

"Bro, it's an autogyro to be precise. A Red Admiral."

"Isn't that a butterfly?"

"A species from your neck of the woods, I know. But their mechanical namesakes are built here on the Big Pumpkin, specifically designed for the local environment."

Zeke whistled. Scuff aimed a key at the bubble, which unlocked with a welcoming beep.

"How much?" Zeke asked, with a rush of guilt.

Scuff threw him a wink. "Used aircraft come very cheap in Mariners Valley. No warranty of course, but it made it all the way from Yuri-Gagarin Freetown."

"The Noctis Labyrinthis is much further Scuff, can—"

"It's the best I could do, bro. Don't get picky on me."

Zeke sighed and scrambled into the dirt-stained interior. The upholstery reeked of Martian beer and tobacco. *Not a good sign*, Zeke thought.

"You do know how to fly this death trap?" he asked.

Scuff gave him his are-you-nuts look. "Sure, with your Albie as automatic pilot."

Although the original Albie had sunk without trace into the quicksand, Zeke had prudently made a back-up copy.

Zeke inserted the back-up disc. Worryingly it took Albie less time to configure the Admiral that it had the Glow-Worm.

"Upgrade Operational, Master Zeke." Albie chimed through the gyro's speakers.

"Albie, launch when ready. Noctis Labyrinthis, maximum speed."

"Affirmative, Master Zeke."

The blades unfurled and began spinning. Every nut, bolt and screw in the Red Admiral rattled ominously. It lifted a few feet. Then, with a sudden, sickening jolt, it lurched back to the ground.

Scuff gasped and Zeke muttered something foul in Hesperian. Principal Lutz was standing where a moment before there was nobody. She had brought them down by sheer willpower. The blades slowed to a halt,

"Bringing a gyro into the School without either a pilot license or a permit from me. Truanting. Putting your lives at risk. I expect this kind of criminal behaviour from Hailey, but you, Mr Barnum, what a bitter disappointment you are."

Scuff hung his head in shame.

"Your School Medal of Honour is hereby rescinded. This time it really is the end, for both of you, regardless of that oafish lieutenant! Give Hailey a free reign, he said. No longer. Zeke Hailey you are once and for all expelled from this School."

To Zeke's surprise her words didn't sting. "You're expelling me?"

"Totally and irrevocably, *mon cherie*."

Zeke felt a gush of excitement. She wasn't vanquishing him, she was liberating him!

"In that case, you old trout, you can go jump in a black hole."

Lutz stared at him as if he were talking in a foreign language. One that even she, the formidable linguist, didn't speak. Zeke turned to his friend.

"Come on Scuff. We've got more important stuff to do."

"Aye, aye Skipper!" Scuff said with a salute.

Still Lutz couldn't fathom what was happening.

"I order you to get out. Out! Out of that silly contraption."

"It's an autogyro, to be precise. Now stand clear, we're taking off."

Lutz's jaw dropped low.

"Mutiny is it? I might have seen it coming. I'll just drag your silly whirligig down."

"And we will take off again. And again. And again. Sooner or later you'll tire and we'll be off. Even you can't hold us down forever."

For the first time in decades Lutz was speechless.

"Oh, by the way, I took photos of Barnside blowing her circuits. Any trouble from you and I'll plaster your illegal android all over the Mars-Wide-Web."

It was a lie but, Zeke fancied, a rather inspired one.

"You wouldn't dare."

"Oh, but I would. I'm expelled, you see. I have absolutely nothing to loose. Tar rah. Albie immediate take off."

Lutz began shouting. But with the blades spinning her words were inaudible. She disappeared from view as the Red Admiral buzzed up into the new Martian day.

Lutz cursed in four languages. Then she looked beyond the departing gyro to the changing sky. A century on Mars had taught the Principal to read its mysterious moods. A whiff of sulphur was blowing up from the distant southern plateaus.

"A turn for the worse," she sighed. "The winds are picking up."

Part Three

Chapter Twenty-Seven

A Hundred Feet Up

The Red Admiral buzzed across a yellow sky. Early morning shadows carpeted the valley floor. Purple canyons soared above the gloom.

The boys' triumph against Principal Lutz left them in cheery spirits. Scuff opened Albie's music files and chose a compilation called 'Three Centuries of Pop'.

"If only I had my guitar!" Scuff said, clicking his fingers to a song about love-struck Fridays.

Later they took turns at pausing Albie and flying the gyro themselves. After a few hair-raising dives, they quickly mastered the joystick, rudders and throttle. Zeke even managed a loop-the-loop.

"Good thing I skipped breakfast!" Scuff grumbled, as they turned right side up.

Later, with the miles clocking up on the gauge, a more serious mood crept over them.

"We're expelled from the best school in the Solar System!" Scuff shouted over the hum of the blades.

"Can't your dad sponsor a new wing? Then the old bat will have to take you back."

"It's not me I'm worried about. How will you get reinstated, never mind track down your father?"

"Scuff, if we don't stop Magma opening the Infinity Trap, none of that will matter anymore."

Scuff frowned. "How can you be so sure?"

Zeke drew a deep breath and began updating the Canadian on his 'trip' inside the engraving.

"How come these things always happen to you?"

"Because I speak Hesperian. And, I think, the Orb of Words somehow made me 'Martian friendly'. Like the engraving knew me."

Scuff chuckled. "The Orb of Words? I like it. A lot catchier than, um, the Globe of Incomprehensible Alien Syntax. Do they come in Spanish? Or Japanese?"

"The Orb is no joke, Scuff."

Scuff lost his smile. "Pardon me, bro. So, this Spiral, is it mega dangerous?"

Zeke stared into the distance. "It's name in Hesperian is *Klriinthnga*. That means Killer Spiral."

"Do these words just pop into your head? You're not communicating with some prehistoric alien ghost, are you?"

"They just pop into my head. And I only understand them if they have a meaning in English. Some words swim about my brain without a shred of meaning. *Mchx-dthfkii*, for example."

"Maybe that means 'the big bad spiral is a wimp'?"

"I wish," Zeke said sadly.

Neither boy said anything for a long time.

"So what's this Infinity Trap like?" Scuff asked eventually.

"Dunno."

"They didn't tell you much, these living thoughts."

"They were recorded before life on Earth existed. It's a miracle they still work."

The gyro juddered over a pocket of warm air.

"What was it like being two dimensional?" Scuff asked.

"Unbelievable."

Scuff picked his nose. "Totally not, bro. You've not been doing your homework."

"Huh?"

"Superstring theory. Its calculations tell us there may be ten or more dimensions all around us. But, being three-dimensional creatures, we can't see them."

Zeke gave him a baffled look.

"Length, width, and height. The three dimensions that shape our awareness of reality. We see atoms as fixed particles in our space-time continuum. Major mistake, bro. They're really strings of energy."

"Like knitting?"

Scuff glared. "Like guitar strings, obviously! Strings vibrating through different universes. We only see a cross section of the greater whole. Anyway, if we are three-dimensional creatures living in a ten-dimensional universe, then being a two dimensional creature is, well, not so inconceivable."

"You're making my head hurt. Change the subject."

"Okay, two more hours and we reach Gagarin Freetown."

A determined look blazed within Zeke's dark eyes, a look Scuff dreaded. "Actually, let's skip it. At this rate we can get to Noctis Labrynthis by tomorrow evening. The Admiral's fusion cells are fully charged."

"No way, bro. I'm not peeing out of a moving aircraft. And my stomach needs regular recharging."

"But Scuff—"

"But-splut, no arguments, bro. I mean it."

Zeke bit deeply on his lower lip. Scuff was risking his life. He had to remember that.

Five golf balls sat on the horizon, arranged in a pentagon. Slowly they grew in into buildings.

"Twenty-first century biospheres, how primitive," Scuff sniffed.

"This place sounds pretty lawless," Zeke remarked.

Scuff flicked a switch on the console. "Albie, are you programmed with the Encyclopaedia Americana?"

"Negative, Sir."

"The Encyclopaedia Marius?"

"Affirmative."

Scuff sighed.

"Everything is so second rate on this planet. Very well, tell us what you know about Yuri-Gagarin. And make it snappy."

Lines of holographic text shimmered in front of the windscreen.

Yuri Gagarin

Born 1934-03-09, Klushino, USSR. Died 1968-03-27. Russian Cosmonaut and first man in space.

Yuri-Gagarin Freetown

A Martian colony that began as a Russian research station in 2124. As the environment in the Mariners Valley stabilised it grew into a significant trading outpost. In 2174 it was decreed a Russian Protectorate. However in 2243 a peaceful revolution, led by Ptolemy Cusp, declared Independence making it the first sovereign state of Mars.

"What a totally jackass name! Who does this Ptolemy Cusp think he is?" Scuff barked.

Albie answered the question with more text.

Ptolemy Cusp

Born 2221-07-08, Hokusai Station, Mars. Un-elected leader of Yuri Gagarin Freetown. 'This young man is a dangerous mix of businessman and revolutionary with a dash of the Samurai for good measure' (Captain Leopold Doughty, the Martian Book of Quotations 2243-14-09)

"It didn't dawn on me there's so much going on outside the School," Zeke said.

"Totally, bro. These so-called Martian trueborns are all for a war of independence, the morons."

"Thought you'd support a war for independence, after all—"

"You're thinking of the American War of Independence, Zeke, I'm from over the border, remember?"

"Oh, sorry." Scuff rolled his eyes and continued, "These trueborns are just troublemakers. How dare they—"

A voice crackled over the radio.

"Autogyro RA1960. Are you landing here?"

"Absolutely," Zeke replied. "Um, permission to land?"

"Permission? Heck boy, you got no horse sense? You don't need no permission. Just park your ve-hee-cle in any free spot you can. See y'all later."

"That's lawless alright." Zeke said, and took control of the joystick

The Red Admiral dropped rapidly over a sea of tents and prefabs. A landing strip opened up in front of them. Zeke steered a perfect touchdown.

"Not bad for a beginner," Scuff muttered, just loud enough to be heard.

A lanky, freckle-faced teenager with black spiky hair ran across the tarmac and tapped on the cockpit. Scuff slid over the windscreen.

"Courtesy of Y.G.F.T.," the older boy drawled in a rich American accent. He handed them canned drinks.

"Craterade, one of our best sellers. Brewed from gen-yoo-ine Martian iron oxide; puts fur on your chest."

A cold drink was exactly what they needed after the long dusty flight. Zeke and Scuff followed the boy back to a flimsy wooden shack with the sign 'Arrival Suite' nailed over its door.

Zeke beamed. "This is a really friendly place."

"Wonder how you go about becoming a citizen?" Scuff retorted.

Both boys squeezed through the narrow entrance. Once inside their smiles evaporated like water on an airless moon. Two burly men in combat fatigues were aiming huge guns at them. A similarly dressed woman stood by the exit. She had tightly-cropped ginger hair and eyes as piercing as spotlights.

"They call me Isla The Incisor, because I'm known for my bite."

She bared two rows of perfect, pearly teeth.

"And I am here, Mr Hailey and Mr Barnum, to arrest you in the name of Ptolemy Cusp."

Chapter Twenty-Eight

The Arrivals Shack

Scuff puffed out his chest as far as it could go. "Listen up, lady, we're on a tight schedule here and need supplies. Keep out of our way. Okay?"

Isla the Incisor clicked her fingers. The Neanderthal on her right aimed his gun, a bulky cylinder of coils and chambers. It began whining.

"Hey! I'm an Canadian citizen!"

A flash of neon ran up the barrel. Scuff covered his eyes. Zeke cried out. And then nothing. Nothing except a whooshing noise.

Zeke raised his eyebrows. "That was a damp squib," he remarked. Scuff let out a sigh of relief.

"Oh was it?" Isla replied with a cunning glint in her eyes. "Okay, psychic boy. Show me your stuff."

Scuff glanced around the room and focused hard on a couple of Craterade cans. Everyone waited for the cans to move. They didn't.

"What have you done to me? My psychokinesis is diddly-squat!"

Isla threw back her head and laughed loudly.

"It's a ferromagnetic gun. It soaked you with magnetic ions, dampening your psychic energies. Don't worry, kid, you'll be back to normal in twenty hours or so."

The boys looked at each other helplessly.

"And if you try any funny business you'll get a blast too," Isla added to Zeke.

Zeke opened his mouth to explain he had no special abilities, but then thought better of it. In any case, supposing he was extrasensory? Scuff certainly seemed to think so.

Isla sat down on the table, resting her feet on the chair.

"Right, to business. Our psychic received a telepathic message this morning about you two."

"Your psychic?" Zeke said in surprise.

"Why not? The governments of Earth don't monopolise all the talent. A man as clever as Ptolemy Cusp is bound to have a psych in his service."

"Sounds like a reject Mariner to me," Scuff said darkly.

"I'll ignore your prejudice. The point is your principal asked us to apprehend you and return you to the Chasm. For your own safety."

"Oh sure," Zeke said, with mock sincerity.

"Apparently Lutz has issued a severe weather warning."

They all turned their heads to the window. There wasn't a cloud in the rusty sky.

"Well, Lutz is the psychic, maybe it's brewing. The point is she wants you back. And Ptolemy owes her a few favours."

"So you're sending us back in chains. What happened to that Freetown spirit?" Zeke asked bitterly.

Isla leaned back. "You have a point, Mr Hailey. Yuri-Gagarin Freetown believes in independence. But we have to coexist with our neighbours peacefully. Nevertheless, Ptolemy instructed me to make you an offer."

"An offer?" Zeke and Scuff said together.

"You're already expelled from the Mariner's school. Come and work with our resident psychic. She's getting on in years. Frankly we'll soon need a successor."

"Ooh! That's an offer with serious potential," Scuff cooed.

"Then it's a yes?"

It sounded too good to be true to Zeke. He scrutinized her face for a hint of deceit. He stared into her flashing blue eyes. Beyond those lay the brain, full of thoughts, memories and feelings. If only he could see into that. If only he could delve just a little deeper.

An image slipped into his mind. A glimpse of a tall, well built Japanese man, a proud and confident man. A man Isla loved. An honest man, but a ruthless one.

Zeke cleared his throat.

"We'd be happy to consider your proposal once we rescue our friend."

"Rescue?"

"Oh I see. This message didn't tell you why we were running away?"

Isla gave them a blank look.

Zeke sucked in a long breath and began...

"Martian monsters kidnapping kids?" Isla exclaimed at the end of the weird tale. "That settles it. You stay with us. This is a conspiracy with the Mariners' fingerprints all over it."

Scuff frowned. "Don't badmouth the Mariners. They're saving mankind."

Isla threw him the oddest look. "Are they? Then why do none of the deep space colonists ever come back? I say the Mariners Institute is up to something. And the Ophir Chasma School is at the rotten core of that plot. You kids are lambs to the slaughter."

"Now you're talking garbage."

"And you're trying my patience. So what's it to be? Shipped back to Earth as delinquents or a lifetime membership in our little freewheeling clan?"

Zeke's mind was in overdrive. The two guns fired magnetism not bullets, but Isla could still detain them by brute force. There was no way he and Scuff could overpower her guards. But they might outrun them. He needed a diversion. Zeke caught Scuff's eye and winked.

"Can we meet this Ptolemy? To help make up our minds?"

Isla beamed.

"Sure." She nodded to one of the security men. "Fetch the electrocabs."

The man left.

"I'm so thirsty, can I have drink?" Zeke asked sweetly.

"Me too," Scuff added.

Isla tossed them the cans of Craterade. Zeke shook his tin vigorously. Scuff copied him.

"What are you doing?" Isla protested.

"THIS!"

Zeke ripped off the can's ring pull. Scuff did the same. Two fountains of brown fizzy pop showered Isla and her thug. They shrieked in disgust.

"RUN!" Zeke cried.

He bolted for the exit back to the runway and grabbed the handle. Desperately he rattled the door in its frame. It was locked from the outside!

"Y'all looking for these?"

They swivelled round to see the spiky-haired teenager sauntering through the front door. He was jangling a ring of keys in his hand.

Zeke muttered a Martian cuss through gritted teeth.

"Good work, Justice," Isla said in a voice as cold as ice.

She slowly wiped the bronze-coloured froth from her face, her pale blue eyes fixed on Zeke and Scuff.

"We're for it now, bro!" Scuff whimpered.

Isla pointed at each of them rapidly with her forefinger. The goon handed his ferromagnetic gun to the boy called Justice, and, dripping soda, pulled out a pair of handcuffs.

"No need for—" Zeke began, as the man seized him, but to no avail. The goon yanked Zeke's wrists behind and clicked the cuffs on. Scuff made a sudden run for the front entrance. In a flash Isla floored him with a karate chop. The goon hauled him up and cuffed him too.

Isla crossed her arms, her face a picture of fury.

"Don't say I didn't try. Let's see what Ptolemy has to say about you two."

"Shucks, can I tag along, Boss?" Justice asked. "Not often we get Mariners in town. I'm mighty curious to learn more."

Isla gave a hard stare as though she thought him an idiot, then nodded. "Whatever, Justice."

At that moment two small, three-wheeled carts pulled up outside.

"My father's golf buggy is more luxurious than that!" Scuff remarked sourly.

"GO!" Isla barked.

The goon gave Zeke a shove in the direction of the door. A picture of Pin-mei, alone in the dark, flashed through his mind. With a heavy heart Zeke walked out into the dust.

Chapter Twenty-Nine

Biosphere Three

"Move!" Isla shouted, prodding Zeke in the back with her ferromagnetic rifle.

The entrance to the white spherical building slid across and the party filed inside. The dusty streets and ramshackle homes of the Freetown disappeared as the door closed behind them. The next door opened into a large hall. An intricately patterned Persian rug led across the chamber, past computer stations and display units stuffed with Oriental antiques, up to the steps of a throne.

The grand wooden seat, engraved with dragons and space rockets, was occupied by a broad-shouldered East Asian man, dressed in a black silk kimono. Ptolemy Cusp, exactly as Zeke had imagined him! A frail, hooded figure, leaning on a walking stick stood beside the great leader. Both were deep in a whispered conversation.

As soon as the great leader saw Isla he gave a click of his fingers. The thin figure bowed and, without turning to reveal his or her face, tottered away into the shadows.

"Isla? Are our visitors now our prisoners?" Ptolemy boomed with a genial grin.

Isla glared at Zeke and approached the throne. She too fell into murmurs and whispers.

Zeke scanned around for an escape route. They were flanked by guards and the teenager Justice. The boy caught Zeke's attention and gave a light-hearted shrug.

"Your hair's bluer than a mountain chickadee. Is that on account of you being a Mariner or did you take a tumble in an ink vat as a young'un?"

"The latter," Zeke replied in a sullen tone.

Justice couldn't stop staring at them. "So y'all have super powers an' all?"

"We prefer the term psychic skills," Scuff said, nose in the air.

"And you Mariners can fly an' all?"

"Depends," Scuff continued.

"Sure would love to see that," Justice said, wide-eyed at the idea.

"Un-cuff me and you will," Zeke suggested, but knew he was grasping at straws.

Justice cackled like a drain. "I may be a country boy but I'm ain't no imbecile!"

"So…where are you from?" Scuff asked.

"Louisiana," Justice replied with pride. "You'll be from the land of moose and maple leaves, I reckon."

Scuff nodded. "You're a long way from the Deep South," he said.

Justice grinned from ear to ear. "You're right. Came here on a school trip. No sooner I'd put foot on dusty soil than I was smitten. Plum fell for the ol' gal."

Zeke and Scuff gave him bewildered looks.

"Why heck, Mars of course! The Big Pumpkin, the Little Kumquat, Dame Ruby, whatever ol' nickname you fancy! I knew in a damn Martian minute this was the place for adventure. Ran away from my dullsville teachers. Bummed around Mariners Valley awhile before destiny washed me up on these far shores. Ol' Mr Cusp gave me a job care-taking his airstrip. And the shack next-door to rest my weary head."

"Don't you miss you parents?" Zeke asked in a horrified voice.

Justice gazed at his enormous feet. "Ain't got none. Never did."

"So why the, if you'll pardon me, unusual name?" Scuff said.

Justice smirked. "All part of being a Freetown citizen. Mr Cusp here says you have to choose a new Martian name and leave your ol' Earth one behind. Symbolic like. I was plain ol' Leroy Planchett till recently."

"But Justice is, well, a tad unusual," Scuff went on, scarcely hiding his scorn.

"Scuff Barnum don't exactly trip off the tongue, now does it. Nope, Justice is what I believe in. Me and the Freetowners. So I took it for my a.k.a."

"You call this justice?" Zeke said bitterly, and jangled his cuffs.

Justice frowned. "Well, it's all part of your adventure, I guess. I envy you for that—chasing off to the boondocks. A gen-yoo-ine damsel in distress. Better than them movies!"

"Then why don't you help us make it a happy ending?" Zeke asked, and jangled his cuff again. Justice simply winked at them, and sidled away among the antique collections.

"He's, how do you say in England, utterly bonkers?" Scuff remarked, rolling his eyes.

Zeke remained silent.

"Here!" Ptolemy Cusp boomed with a grand wave.

The two boys approached, heads lowered. The great man studied his captives for a moment, and nodded to the guard to unlock their cuffs.

"Those things are tight," Scuff complained, massaging each wrist in turn.

"No more tricks, huh boys? We're all grown-ups here, aren't we?" Ptolemy said.

The Freetown leader had deep-set eyes and wide cheekbones. His easy smile revealed large, snow white teeth. He had the air of a man as much at home on a battlefield as a library. Despite himself, Zeke warmed to the leader of Freetown.

"Correct me if I'm wrong," Ptolemy said. "You're on a mission to rescue a friend from that maniac Magma and he's armed himself with some kind of Hesperian technology?"

"In a nutshell, bro," Scuff replied.

Ptolemy sent Isla a look. "Hesperian technology? How interesting." He returned his attention back to the boys. "Don't take this the wrong way, but you two youngsters are alone on a hostile world. We've heard nasty rumours about Magma's dig. People disappearing. You'd have a much greater chance of success accompanied by, shall we say, a crack team of commandoes."

Isla's mouth dropped. "Tolly—I mean Sir, you're not suggesting…?"

"I am indeed, Isla. Don't let the Craterade incident fool you boys. Isla and her team are tough cookies."

"That I know," Scuff muttered, patting his bruised stomach.

Ptolemy let out a loud guffaw. "So we're agreed! Isla will escort you."

"And what do you want in return?" Zeke asked softly.

Ptolemy beamed at him. "All I ask is, after the rescue of your lady friend, you give some serious thought to joining the Unpro."

Zeke and Scuff stared at him.

"Oh I see," he went on. "You new arrivals aren't familiar with Martian politics yet. Allow me to enlighten you. Every colony, outpost or damn weather station on this lump of rock is under the protection of one Earth superpower or another."

"Oh, you mean the protectorates?" Scuff said.

Ptolemy nodded. "Tithonium is a protectorate of the United Nations. The Chinese have Hellas Planitia. The Americans have their flag dotted everywhere, and so on. Even your School is a protectorate of the Mariners Institute."

Zeke stroked his chin. "And Yuri Gagarin Freetown used to be a Russian Protectorate, but you declared independence and—"

"Broke free, as any child must from their parent if they are to grow up. And our example has inspired settlers everywhere. We've given birth to the Unpro movement, the Unprotected. The True Martian Nation."

"The Unpro sound like a bunch of troublemakers to me," Scuff said with a frown.

Ptolemy's smile never wavered. "Spoken like a child of Earth. But if you'd grown up here, like me, you'd feel differently. Mars for the true-borns. That's the revolution coming, boys, and you two have a chance to join the winning side."

"Why can't Earth and Mars just get along?" Zeke piped up.

Anger clouded Ptolemy's handsome face. "Mars isn't a lifeboat planet. It can't take everyone escaping Earth's environmental mess. It's time for Mars to be more selective. But you can benefit from that."

"Really, how exactly?" Zeke asked, unable to hide his curiosity.

Ptolemy's charming smile returned. "I advise you to think of the future, Mr Hailey. A friend in high places could come in very useful one day. I could get your family through the Office of Martian Naturalisation and Immigration with a word in the right ear."

The word 'family' burned in Zeke's ears. His father! He had completely forgotten about his missing father. Zeke's future, if he had one, wasn't going to revolve around an independent Mars. The great leader's proposal was useless to him.

"And if we say no to your offer?"

The great leader sighed. "Then regrettably I must hand you over to the Mariners. Lutz and I go back a long way. Longer than you could imagine."

Zeke knew what he had to do.

"OK, we accept."

"We do?" Scuff gasped. "Oh, yes we do."

"When will we be ready to leave?" Zeke asked.

Ptolemy gestured at Isla.

She scratched her ginger scalp. "A cross-valley mission? I think we could be ready in four days. But that tinplated gyro only seats two, so then another nine days to reach the Noctis Labrynthis on foot."

"So be it. Till then I advise you two to rest. We have some guest rooms at the top of Biosphere Two. Isla can escort you."

"Sir, shouldn't we take some precautions?" Isla asked, with a filthy look at Zeke.

Ptolemy threw his head back and laughed heartily. "Isla! The Freetown runs on trust. We must put faith in Zeke and his friend."

Zeke pursed his lips. Surely it wasn't going to be that easy?

"Oh, one last little thing," Ptolemy said, as the boys turned to leave.

"We'll need the key to your Red Admiral. Just so Justice can service it, you understand."

Zeke and Scuff exchanged looks.

"Oh sure," Zeke said with a forced smile, and handed over the key.

Chapter Thirty

Biosphere Two

The biosphere door swished open.

"This is totally nuts," Scuff whispered, as he peered over Zeke's shoulder. Outside, beyond the doorway, the Freetown lay sleeping. The sea of shacks and tents and crates was dark and still.

"Why don't we take up Ptolemy's offer?" he went on.

Zeke sniffed. "We don't have time, Scuff. And I don't trust him. The way he's set himself up as the Emperor of Freetown. The look on his face when we mentioned Hesperians."

Scuff chuckled. "The Emperor of Freetown. It fits. Still, I couldn't help but like him."

"Me too, but this revolution is all that matters to him. We'd be pawns."

"So you really think we can get into Justice's shack and find the key?"

Zeke stuck out his chin. "We have to try."

He stepped out into the night. An ear–splitting siren erupted.

"Oops! An infrared tripwire!" Scuff gasped, glancing down at the bottom of the doorway.

"RUN!" Zeke barked.

They sprinted across the dusty courtyard.

"Where now!" Scuff squawked.

Zeke desperately turned from right to left. Which way led back to the airstrip? The siren continued wailing. The nearest tents were lighting up.

No, no, no, thought the little voice inside Zeke's head. *We mustn't fail!*

At that moment an electrocab sped out from the shadows and pulled up in a flurry of dirt.

"Shucks, you two just can't keep out of trouble," Justice said with an amiable chuckle. He pointed to the backseat. "Make with the hasty exit, boys! Before Isla and her goons come a-swarming like flies to a stale burger!"

Zeke and Scuff needed no encouragement. They leapt into the rear of the cab and Justice stepped on the accelerator. The wheels shrieked. The electrocab zoomed forward into the forest of tents. Zeke grabbed onto the handrails and glanced back. Another cab was hurtling after them! He couldn't make out the figures clearly, but Isla's voice rang shrill and clear above the din of the alarm.

"STOP IN THE NAME OF PTOLEMY CUSP!"

"Faster!" Zeke cried to Justice, as the three-wheeler lurched over bump after bump.

The path weaved deeper into the maze of makeshift homes. At every turn they narrowly missed a canvas-side or a tent peg.

Justice hooted like a frog. "Sure is fun!" he cackled.

"Why are you helping us?" Scuff asked, his voice wobbling with the shudder of the cab.

"Heck, why not?" Justice replied. "Life was getting dull. I fancied a shakedown."

"Justice, you can't come with us," Zeke said sadly. "There isn't room in the Admiral."

"Tell me something I don't know!" Justice called back.

"But, won't Isla throw you in the slammer?" Scuff asked.

Justice laughed again. "Slammer? What slammer? You need civilisation for a jail, boys. In case you ain't noticed, Yuri-Gagarin Freetown is anything but!"

Zeke steadied himself against the rails. "What will happen to you?"

"Aw, don't worry about me," Justice replied. "A slapped wrist, a smack on the bee-hind, it'll come right, y'all see."

Zeke and Scuff exchanged disbelieving looks.

Justice said, "You boys are on an adventure. The whole damn sake of why I ran away was for adventure. I just gotta help, or my name ain't Justice Leroy Planchett."

The way ahead suddenly cleared to reveal the airstrip and its tiny shack, dwarfed beneath the vast night sky.

Justice hit the brakes, throwing the boys off the backseat. They landed on the cabin floor with a hard thump.

"Oh, catch!" the older boy said, and tossed Zeke the key to the red admiral.

Zeke clambered out and shook Justice by the hand as forcefully as he could. The words he wanted to say didn't come, so instead he mumbled a simple, "thank you."

Justice's eyes gleamed with fire. "Y'all go get yer lady friend. I'll put a spanner in dear ol' Isla's works."

He revved up the engine and the vehicle zoomed around and back into the shacks.

Zeke and Scuff sprinted across the tarmac. The loud sound of two unseen electrocabs colliding brought them to a temporary standstill. Shouting and cursing rang through the crisp air.

Zeke picked up his pace again, aiming the key at the gyro. The admiral beeped into life.

"Albie open up!" Zeke shouted.

The windscreen slid over. The boys jumped into their seats. Zeke rammed the key into the ignition slot.

"Emergency launch," he yelled.

The blades started to hum. One of Isla's security men loomed out of nowhere, nearly upon them. The Red Admiral lifted a few inches. The man leapt onto the fuselage but with nothing to grip, slid off. The gyro turned away from the landing strip and ascended, up into the glittering stars.

Chapter Thirty-One

Ius Chasma

Zeke peered through the windscreen into an ocean of night. Not a single photon lamp challenged its dominion over Mars. Earth was this way once, he thought, before the invention of electricity. Not the glittering diamond of today, but dark as a lump of coal.

It was three A.M. They had flown non-stop since escaping Yuri-Gagarin. It was Zeke's turn to keep an eye on the autopilot. Scuff was snoring loudly beside him.

"This is about as much fun as Quantum Physics!" Zeke grumbled.

He tuned into Mars Valley Radio, the only station on the planet. He wanted to catch the news for any mention of bad weather. But all he heard were the latest terra-forming reports. Oxygen levels were up but air pressure was down. Crop yields were stable but immigration was rocketing.

"Lutz is lying through her teeth." Zeke remarked to himself.

After the bulletin the DJ came on the air.

"This is Raymond Gamma the Third, the man who puts the crackle in the airwaves, here with another all night play list of Country classics. Country and Martian that is."

A slow, twangy serenade filled the cockpit. Zeke was exhausted. Listening to the soothing guitar chords he leant back and picked out his favourite constellations. There was Cygnus, Cassiopeia and Cepheus, all flickering like candles. He decided to rest his eyes. Just for a minute...

*H*e was running. Running and leaping pools of fiery lava. His chest pounded with fear. He glanced back. A vast nebula was gobbling up the horizon. A moon-sized phenomena in the shape of a spiral. His father leapt out from the surrounding flames, reaching out to save him. But, with an agonising scream, Hailey Senior flew into the air, snatched by a jagged tentacle.

"WAKE UP!"

It was morning. Scuff was shaking him by the shoulder.

"LOOK!"

Scuff pointed to the south. A long, mud-coloured cloud stretched over the canyon ridges.

"It's a sandstorm! We gotta land!" Scuff wailed.

"No! Pin's life depends on us. Everyone's does."

Scuff ignored him. "Albie, is there any place we can sit out the storm?"

"The storm will cross our flight path before we reach a colony. Recommend we shelter in the lee of Geryon Montes."

This was the mountainous curtain of rock to their north, cutting the Ius Chasma off from the neighbouring canyon.

"Only till the storm passes," Scuff implored.

Their eyes met. Zeke's burned with determination. The same determination that had brought him all the way to Mars.

"Albie, whose voice do you obey?"

"Yours, Master Zeke."

"Good. Ignore any command from Scuff and continue on course to the Noctis Labrynthis."

"You'll kill us both, you nutcase."

Zeke glared at his best friend.

"*Trp yaa t-th,*" he said darkly.

"The same to you with ribbons," Scuff retorted fiercely, and looked away.

The sandstorm grew. With alarming speed it reached across Mariners Valley, obscuring the sky. Invisible waves of turbulence reached ahead of the cloud front and buffeted the gyro. The boys bounced inside like peas in a rattle.

"PLEASE LAND!" Scuff shrieked.

"WE'LL RIDE IT OUT."

"WE WON'T!"

The towering wall of dirt and dust bore down upon them. Zeke stared up at its shapeless crests, racing towards them like demon horses. His heart sank.

"Um, maybe I made a—"

Before he could finish the tsunami cloud struck. A cascading brown haze blotted out the daylight. A gale shook the gyro violently. Lightning flashed deep in the storm's angry heart.

"LAND, LAND, LAND!" Zeke shouted.

He was too late. A bolt of electricity, generated by the friction of a trillion sand particles, licked the propeller. It exploded. The Admiral plummeted.

"USE YOUR POWERS, ZEKE. LIKE THE SYCAMORE," Scuff cried.

Zeke was about to beg Scuff to use his. Then he remembered Isla had soaked Scuff with magnetism, temporarily erasing his psychic skills. Only Zeke could save them.

A world of gusting sand howled outside. Everything was confusion. The seething chaos only distracted him. Zeke closed his eyes and took deep measured breaths. Old Flounder's words echoed in his mind.

Visualise and realise. Thought is the most powerful force in the Universe.

Zeke pictured the falling craft. He imagined his hands surrounding the scorched fuselage and holding it tightly. His scalp tingled, as if energy was pouring from every pore. Their rate of descent began to slow. He'd done it!

SMASH!!!

They collided against an outcrop of rock, crumpling the gyro's hull. It ricocheted away like a pinball.

CRASH!

They smacked into the ground at a shallow angle and kept rolling. Over and over and over. And then nothing.

⬤⬤⬤⬤⬤⬤

"**I**mmediate evacuation recommended."

The blood-red mist cleared from Zeke's sight. The Admiral had landed on its back. The console was suspended above him, spitting sparks.

Albie continued, "Fusion cells leaking. Fire is ninety three percent probable."

Zeke struggled to undo his safety harness. His shoulder was wet and his left hand throbbing. He summoned all his willpower and pushed the pain from his mind. He turned to Scuff.

"COME ON!"

Scuff was slumped away from him, motionless.

"SCUFF WE'VE GOT TO GO!"

Scuff remained silent and still. Anger surged through Zeke's body.

"THIS IS NO TIME TO SULK! BLAME ME LATER!"

Zeke sidled towards his friend, fuming at his attitude. In the flickering light, he saw Scuff's face. The Canadian was unconscious. Blood was trickling down his bruised cheeks.

Time froze.

Yes, you did this. Now you save him.

A burning smell clawed at Zeke's nostrils.

"Albie, what should I do?"

"Suggest withdrawal to unidentified building. Six hundred and fifty yards at two o'clock. Utilise emergency kit to maximize survival."

"What kit?"

A box beneath the console popped open.

"Thanks, Albie."

"Master Zeke, circuits contaminated. Must close to avoid irreparable—"

Albie's tinny voice died.

Desperately, Zeke rifled the kit and plucked out the night vision goggles. Would they see through a sand blizzard as well as the dark? He pushed on the fractured windscreen. It didn't budge. The cockpit was heating up. An image of the two of them in flames seared through Zeke's brain.

Don't panic, warned his inner voice.

With all his strength he pressed against the windscreen. Again zilch.

Think Fool!

The latch! Zeke reached across and tugged at the lever. The windscreen half opened. The storm ripped into the cockpit. At least the goggles kept the sand out of his eyes.

"Urgh!" he grunted, throwing an aching shoulder against the glass. Inch by inch he forced back the screen. Next he knelt down and unbuckled Scuff. He feared he was making his friend's injuries worse by moving him, but they had to get out. An acrid reek of melting plastic was filling the Admiral.

Straining beneath Scuff's weight Zeke lifted him up and out. Next, Zeke clambered up into the roaring weather. He lowered Scuff onto the ground. Jumping down, Zeke hoisted Scuff over his shoulders and staggered a few steps. His knees buckled under the weight. He just wasn't strong enough. It was useless.

"SCUFF WAKE UP!"

No response.

Come on, use that brain!

The gyro seats! He dived back into the cockpit. Frantically he reached underneath the upholstery, searching for the lever that would release his chair. The console was giving off enough heat to fry eggs. There was the lever! He tossed the freed seat out of the wreckage.

Wait!

Wait for what? Of course, the emergency kit! He hastily emptied its contents into his backpack. One more precious thing needed saving. Albie! He prised Albie's disc from the hot machinery and dropped that in too. Flames erupted. In his haste to get out Zeke gashed his thigh against the broken glass of the windscreen.

Out in the deafening, battering, stinging wind Zeke flattened out the seat. It became a sled with Scuff secured in its safety harness. But which way was the building? Albie had said two o'clock. If the nose of the gyro was twelve then two had to be in that direction.

"Kshgthgaa!" he cursed.

He had nothing to pull Scuff's seat. The only way to move was backwards, bending over the seat and tugging by the harness. The discomfort added to his pain.

Serves you right.

Zeke trudged off in what he hoped was the right direction. He took one last look at the red admiral. Flames were dancing from the cockpit. Then the storm obscured it forever.

Chapter Thirty-Two

Location unknown

The sandstorm gnawed at his face. Pain raced from his wrist to his shoulder. His back ached from the constant bending and the cut in his thigh throbbed. But Zeke didn't cry. The sight of his unconscious friend stalled any tears.

Zeke straightened his back and checked their bearings. He could see nothing but swirling sand through the green phosphor of his NVGs. But a miniature radar inside the goggles was registering a building-sized bleep.

An outline formed through the dust clouds. That was it! With renewed energy Zeke grabbed the reins of the seat and hurried on.

He came to a steel-ringed entrance. An airlock. This meant the place predated Martian terra-forming and had to be over a hundred years old. But the airlock was wide open. Zeke's heart sunk. Was the structure abandoned?

He hauled his friend through the depressurisation chamber into a ready room. As Zeke left the storm behind his NVGs began functioning more clearly. He could make out the pegs where pressure suits once hung. Each peg had a name card.

A long corridor littered with debris ran away into pea-coloured darkness.

"HELLO!" Zeke shouted. He listened keenly for a reply. None came, other than the moaning of the gale.

It was still too windy. He pulled Scuff through the nearest door into some kind of office. A large empty desk dominated the room and there were shelves and filing cabinets. The windows were shuttered. A thick layer of dirt covered everything.

Zeke closed the door. At last relief from the elements. He retraced his steps through the filth to his friend.

Scuff made a pathetic sight. His hair was matted with sand and blood. His face was dirty and swollen.

"What have I done to you?"

A terrible thought suddenly gripped Zeke. How did he know Scuff wasn't dead? Zeke threw himself down and placed a hand on Scuff's chest. With a sigh of relief Zeke found a steady rise and fall. He examined the head wound. The bleeding had stopped, in fact the airborne sand had helped it clot.

Next Zeke sorted through his backpack.

"Rotten second-hand survival kits!" he cursed.

There was no rescue beacon, nor any medical supplies or food. It did contain a foil blanket which he tucked over Scuff. Other than this, most of the items were useless: a bottle opener, a cigarette lighter, cards and toiletries.

"What kind of emergency are these for?" Zeke wondered aloud.

CLICK.

Zeke wheeled round. The door had shut! Yet hadn't he already closed it? Zeke leapt to the door and opened it. He peered down the corridor into the darkness. No one.

"HELLO? ANYONE THERE?"

Nothing stirred but the sand, billowing in from outside. Obviously the door had simply blown ajar. Zeke was letting his imagination run away with itself. He turned back into the room and stopped dead in his tracks.

A book was sitting on the desk. But when he had first entered the room the desktop was bare. An icy sensation crawled the length of Zeke's spine. He checked the corridor a second time. Gloom, drifting sand, broken sticks of furniture, and nothing alive.

Zeke closed the door very tightly. Peering through his NVG's he inspected the book. It was leather bound and embossed on the front.

Beagle UK Research Station Logbook. Year 2090

Zeke skimmed through the handwritten pages. It was exactly as it said on the cover, the journal of a research team stationed there one hundred and sixty odd years before. Most of the daily entries were signed by a Dr Tom Ganister and recorded the various experiments by his colleagues. Occasionally the handwriting changed, when a Dr Jed Wiley or a Dr Veronica Skye took turns to pen the reports.

That lump of ice seemed to have lodged at the base of Zeke's skull. There was something spooky about reading the words of the long dead. He glanced at the door. It remained as he left it.

He continued flicking through the well-thumbed pages. An unusually short entry caught his attention.

July 12th
This is the most amazing day of my life! Silverman and Welt found something.

They were digging for possible uranium deposits, after the Geiger counter picked up high radiation. Instead they unearthed a perfectly formed stone sphere carved with unfathomable markings. Something made, not natural.

The entire team are buzzing. Have we uncovered evidence of Martians? This discovery could change everything!
Dr Tom Ganister.

Zeke wolf-whistled softly. Had he stumbled on a record of the finding of the first ever Hesperian artefact? And it sounded very much like the Orb of Words. This journal might be of tremendous historical significance.

A noise outside disturbed Zeke's concentration. Just the weather, he told himself and returned to tattered pages.

The entries became more irregular after July twelfth. Pages were torn out, others were heavily stained. Zeke picked one at random.

Aug 2nd

The sphere's missing! Wheeler went to lab 4 after breakfast and the containment unit was empty. Unlocked! I've searched the base and nothing. It has to be stolen, but who? And why?

"Uhhh…"

Zeke dropped the book in fright. It was only Scuff, vomiting onto the floor. Zeke knelt beside him.

"How are you feeling, um, bro?"

"Like a meteor impact crater…crashed."

He slumped back into unconsciousness. If only they had water and food. Zeke cursed their bad luck. They were trapped in a remote location in a hurricane which could last days. Scuff had a serious concussion. And it was all Zeke's fault.

Think, think!

Could there be anything salvageable in the station? Dr Ganister's team had lived there one and a half centuries before. But maybe others had been there in the ensuing years? Supposing there was some food to be left behind? After all, organic matter lasted much longer on Mars, due to the low levels of bacteria, fungi and humidity. A brief image of his mummified body being found by future explorers sneaked into Zeke's mind.

"Where's my stiff upper lip when I need it!"

Zeke made a mental list of what to look for: preserved foods, bottled water, a radio, a heat source. He propped Scuff on his side, in case he threw up again. Zeke took a deep breath and left the office.

The corridor branched out in two opposing directions. Zeke rubbed the grime from a sign on the wall. To the left were the laboratories and research facilities. To the right were the living quarters and kitchen. That sounded more promising.

The passage was cluttered with all kinds of junk. Zeke squeezed around broken chairs, wooden crates, bits of machinery. What on Earth, or rather, what on Mars had happened here? Perhaps gangs from the mining companies had ransacked the place. Zeke had been on the planet long enough to know of their terrible reputation. Or had the citizens from Gagarin Freetown stripped the valuables? Living in the bleak Mariners Valley taught everyone the value of recycling.

He focused his NVGs through an open doorway. The interior was nothing but a murky emptiness. Another sign proclaimed this was the kitchen.

Don't go in!

Zeke suppressed his inner voice. There was no such things as bogeymen, ghosts or…well, now he came to think of it, there were Martians. Zeke had come face to face with the Dust Devil. If that had survived through the millennia, who knows what else had?

"Anyone there? I come in, um, peace."

Silence. Even the wailing of the storm had faded. Zeke reminded himself of Scuff's injury and stepped into the blackness.

The vague shapes of storage containers and refrigerators emerged from the nothingness. His foot kicked against something metal that skidded away. Probably a cooking utensil.

Zeke swung slowly round, trying to make sense of the jumbled scene. Then, there among the straight lines of the kitchen, he spied something curved. Something crouching in a corner. Something with eyes.

Zeke fled. He scrambled back down the passage, banging against the maze of hardware. His heart was in his throat. His lungs worked overtime. He raced back to the main corridor.

THUMP!

Zeke ran head first into a huge, shadowy figure.

Chapter Thirty-Three

The Abandoned Research Station

The broad shape pinned Zeke's arms to his ribcage. With only his legs free Zeke kicked like a mule.

"Stop struggling or I'll smack you."

He gazed into the face of his assailant. Even though the man's eyes were hidden behind NVG's, Zeke recognised the moustache and strong cheekbones.

"Lieutenant Doughty?"

"One and the same, boy."

"What are you doing here?"

Doughty released his iron grip. "Rescuing you. And why the hell are you running like that?"

"There's something after me. A monster."

They both glanced down the dark corridor. Nothing.

"The storm's got you spooked, kiddo."

"How did you find us?"

"Radar. Ultra-wideband of course. Capable of detecting a flea up a dog's backside from fifty miles."

"I have to get to the Noctis Labyrinthis."

"Then meet the Noctis Labyrinthis express."

Zeke's jaw dropped.

"Young man, I'm putting a stop to Magma's plot."

Finally! Someone believed him.

"So where's the fat boy?"

"In there. Concussion."

"I see. Best we leave him here. I'll radio his coordinates back to HQ. They'll send a med team."

"Lieutenant Doughty, Sir, we can't leave Scuff behind."

"Where we're going is too dangerous for an invalid. He stays."

Zeke's mind raced. The future of all mankind depended on stopping Magma. What was more important than that? Yet could he leave his best friend, alone and injured, in this ill-fated ruin?

"Sir, I'd better stay. I'm responsible for Scuff's condition."

Doughty was silent for a moment. Zeke gazed into the blank NVGs and wondered what the soldier was thinking.

"Never leave a comrade behind. Very commendable. Come on then, my Bronto's outside. The fastest, toughest transport on Mars."

Zeke half-expected a robotic dinosaur as he helped Scuff stagger outside. Instead he found a gigantic torpedo-shaped vehicle on caterpillar tracks.

"Open up," Doughty barked above the choking winds.

A circular hatch slid across. The boys climbed into a warm chamber heavy with the smells of coffee and bacon. They collapsed onto a soft, welcoming couch.

"This is the ready room. To the back is the fusion core. I'd keep out of there if I were you. Up front is the Bridge. You fix yourselves some rations while I get cruise control sorted."

Doughty squeezed himself out through the bulkheads.

"Food! Now!" Scuff snorted.

"You're clearly on the road to recovery." Zeke smiled and busied himself in the kitchen. A low pumping noise reverberated through the steel walls before a sudden lurch threw Zeke against the cold fusion oven.

"We're off then!" he said.

"FOOD!"

Soon they were devouring toasted bacon sandwiches.

Scuff eyed Zeke angrily. "Strictly speaking, I'm not speaking to you, bro. You nearly killed me."

Zeke lowered his head. "You're totally right. I made a pig's ear of the whole thing."

"A pig's ass is a better comparison, don't you think?"

"Is there anything I can do to make it up?"

Scuff chewed thoughtfully on a mouthful. "I'll let you know when I think of something. In the meantime I forgive you, seeing we're on a mission to save mankind."

Zeke sighed with relief. "How's the head wound?"

"Tender as a newborn babe. Do I look anywhere near as bad as you?"

Zeke observed his reflection in his knife. His clothes were spotted with blood and his cheeks were raw, as though scrubbed with sandpaper. "I cut my thigh in the crash, but it's not serious. The sandstorm burned our faces."

Doughty called to them. Gulping down the last of the grub they hurried to the Bridge.

"Wow!" Zeke cried, gawping at all the beeping and bleeping hardware. Although the Bridge was smaller than he expected, it was clearly state of the art. Doughty sat before a series of screens, digital, infra red, thermal, radar, sonar and several more beyond Zeke's knowledge. Everywhere else was crammed with computers. Doughty glanced at them impatiently.

"Take these nano-pills to speed up the healing process. You boys have some nasty scratches. And these green ones are painkillers."

The boys swallowed the drugs.

"Why is it called a Bronto?" Scuff enquired.

"Biometric Rapid Overland Environmental Theatre of Operations."

"That doesn't spell Bronto, Captain," Scuff replied.

Doughty gave him a cold look. "There's an N in environment, I believe, and it's Lieutenant."

"Pardon me, Mr Lieutenant, SIR!" Scuff gave a sarcastic salute.

"What does biometric mean?" Zeke said, hastily changing the subject.

"This Bronto only responds to me, my retinal scans, my DNA or my voice patterns. In case of capture the enemy can't do squat with it."

"Cool."

Scuff had more questions. "So why were you tracking—" but before he could finish a yawn overwhelmed him.

"Two naughty runaway boys? I've had Zeke under surveillance since we first met."

Zeke frowned. Doughty's tone wasn't as friendly as usual. Scuff was obviously annoying him. Scuff annoyed a lot of people. Zeke shifted uneasily.

"Scuff. We ought to thank Leopold for saving our—"

Scuff dropped like a brick onto the floor.

"He's sick!" Zeke shouted.

"Not at all, healthy as a barnyard animal. It's the knockout drops."

Their eyes met. Zeke's brain couldn't process the words he was hearing.

"Knockout drops?"

Doughty gave a sadistic smirk. "Three, two, one and goodnight."

Zeke felt himself falling into a bottomless pit. Then came unconsciousness.

For a sickening moment Zeke thought he was in a coffin. Then he realised it was a kind of sleeping berth. He was lying on a hard mattress, with the upper bunk a few inches above his head. To his right was a porthole, revealing the orange haze outside. On his left was a long hatch. He pushed it back and slipped out into a narrow aisle lined with more berths. This led back to the Ready Room.

Scuff stood at the grill, with his back towards Zeke, frying eggs.

"The toilet's that away." He pointed to a small concertina door. No sooner had he said those words than an urge gripped Zeke to empty his bowels.

A few minutes later Zeke hurried back, hands dripping with soapy water.

"What's going on?"

Scuff turned around with a plateful of eggs on toast. He had the nastiest black eye Zeke had ever seen. The eyelid was puffed up and the colour of beetroot.

"Get this down you. Mom always says a good meal helps in a crisis."

Scuff sank into a chair and burst into tears. Zeke's appetite died. He waited for his friend to calm down.

"He did it, didn't he?"

Scuff made a brave effort to rein in his feelings. "I woke an hour ago. I banged and screamed on the door, which was locked, till Doughty came and 'subdued' me."

"Why is he doing this? Why did he drug us?"

"Oh, about that. We've been out for two days."

"TWO DAYS!"

"Those so-called painkillers are some kind of military drug. Doughty called them a 'chemical restraint'. They also slow down your bodily functions until you come to. That's why you needed the bathroom pretty damn quick."

"And the nano-pills?"

"At least he wasn't lying about that. The gash on my head is fading and the headache's all gone. Well it was till he whacked me half way across this deck."

"Couldn't you use your mind powers and crown him with the frying pan?"

"Good old Lieutenant Doughty has a strong magnetic field resonating throughout the Bronto. Our powers are useless."

The two boys exchanged looks. A feeling of defeat seeped into Zeke's heart.

"Zeke, we're dead meat."

The circular hatch to the bridge unscrewed. Doughty stepped inside. His presence dwarfed everything else. He had a gun in one hand while two peculiar objects dangled from the other. They were head cages, metal baskets that strapped around the neck.

"Put them on," Doughty snarled, and threw the cages on the table.

Zeke jumped up. "WHY ARE YOU DOING THIS?"

Doughty's arm swung with the speed of a tiger's paw. The back of his hand caught Zeke's cheek. Zeke crumpled like paper. The man's strength was terrifying.

"Little boys should be seen and not heard, got it?"

As Zeke jumped up, Doughty motioned at the masks with his gun. The boys slipped them on, and took turns to padlock the other's neck strap.

"A simple idea. Imprison those gifted brains of yours in magnetised iron and blank out your creepy powers."

Zeke drew a deep breath. "You've been working with Magma right from the start. The whole visit to the School, making sure I was left alone with him, then conveniently saving me. A dirty trick."

Doughty stroked his square chin with the barrel of his gun. "It was Magma's idea. I wanted to torture the information out of you. But Tiberius suggested our little charade. Better you spill the beans voluntarily to dear old Uncle Leopold. Then the old fool nearly gave the game away. Greeting me as someone he knew after I told you I'd never met him. But you were too busy being our pawn to notice. Now you've unlocked the Infinity Trap for us."

He turned towards the main exit. "Open outer hatch."

There was a grinding metallic noise and a shaft of pale light sliced into the Bronto.

Doughty bowed with mock humility. "Welcome to the Noctis Labyrinthis."

Chapter Thirty-Four

Magma's Base Camp

The boys stepped into the orange sunlight and looked around. After four weeks in Mariners Valley Zeke was accustomed to five-mile-high canyons. But at the Noctis Labyrinthis those walls merged. Only a hundred feet separated the two twisting cliffs, each soaring heavenwards.

A wave of vertigo flooded over Zeke. He lowered his gaze sharply and focused on the ground. They were surrounded by tents, boxes of equipment, and dented old solar scooters. The site appeared deserted.

Two men in Tithonium military garb and carrying rifles sauntered from the nearest tent. They saluted Doughty with a "yo!"

"Regan, Howard, at ease," he said. "Men, meet two of the biggest pains in our collective Martian butt. If they give you any trouble put a few air holes in those obstinate skulls."

The two thugs leered like crocodiles.

"Yoo-hoo!"

It was Professor Magma, emerging from the largest tent with a glass of champagne in hand. He was followed by Trixie Cutter, swigging from the bottle, and an uneasy-looking Snod. They were dressed in hiking gear.

"Well, quite the cosy reunion." Magma giggled as he drew close.

"As cosy as a pack of hyenas," Zeke snarled. POW!

Regan rammed Zeke in the gut with his rifle. Zeke fell to his knees.

"Now, now," Magma chirped. "This is a day for rejoicing. Keep a civil tongue in that bratty head of yours."

"Rejoicing for what?" Scuff asked dourly.

"The dawn of a new era, naturally. The first day of the Tiberian Empire."

Zeke pulled himself up. "How will you achieve that exactly?"

Magma sighed. "Frankly, I'm disappointed. I thought you, our freaky little Hesperian, would figure it out. This is the day we open the Infinity Trap, a day that will shine forever."

"And release the Spiral?"

"Exactly, the Infinity Trap opens a path to the Spiral."

"What makes you think the Spiral will help you?"

Magma gave a haughty laugh. "You make it sound like a person. The Spiral is an energy source of unimaginable power. I'm going to tap into that power and become a living God. My rule will bring peace and happiness for all. I'll be known as Tiberius, Saviour of Humanity."

Doughty coughed loudly. "While saving me the biggest pay cheque in history."

"And me!" Trixie piped in. "It was me who lured the little girl out to your ambush."

"You started with Pin because she saw what was coming," Zeke said with a fierce scowl.

Magma grinned. "True, I couldn't have her spilling any ancient Martian beans. After that I had the Dust Devil sniff out the most talented. Excluding Trixie of course."

"You don't know what you're getting into!" Zeke protested.

Magma glared at him. "How dare you speak to a man of my genius with such insolence. I've been studying Hesperian secrets for years now. He who opens the Infinity Trap absorbs its infinite energy. That's their legacy."

"You're wrong!" Zeke cried.

Another POW! Zeke writhed in the dirt. Yet nobody had moved.

Trixie, eyes aglow, smiled sweetly. "Forgive me. I can't stand disobedient Earthworms."

"An army of you and I could take the solar system." Doughty smirked and threw her a wink.

"Well let's press on," Magma said. "Leopold, if you will."

The Lieutenant fished a key from his pocket and undid Scuff's head cage. Magma produced a small gadget, resembling a digital tin opener.

"A psychometer," he explained, pressing it against Scuff's temple.

"For measuring psychic brainwaves?" Scuff asked.

"Very good. This one's been gathering dust in Lutz's desk for years."

"I bet she happily…gave it…to you," Zeke gasped from the ground, clutching his bruised stomach.

His captors broke into side-splitting laughter.

"You moron. I stole it from her," Trixie guffawed.

A sharp pang struck Zeke's heart. "But the meeting? She's in on the whole thing!"

Trixie placed a delicate foot on his ribcage. "That old bat proved a bigger dupe than you. We buttered her up to get the Professor into the School. Gave her a spiel about sponsoring poor kids and stuff."

Zeke swore. All this time he'd been wrong.

Magma slipped on his glasses and examined Scuff's results.

"Hmm. I see you're a telepathist."

"What? Psychokinesis is my best suit!"

"Sorry, but reading minds is what you're good at, and even then you're rather mediocre."

Scuff flushed. "I'm a certified gifted child. That gadget's dysfunctional."

Doughty snapped the head cage back in place.

"Stand up," Magma ordered Zeke.

He staggered to his feet, still winded from the last blow.

Now comes the moment of truth, he thought. *Proof beyond doubt that I'm a fraud.*

The metal headgear was unbuckled. Magma pressed the cold steel of the psychometer against Zeke's forehead. Instantly it whirred, clicked and pinged. Magma held the readout up to his eyes and whistled.

Trixie grabbed it from him. "Fatty's right. It's broken."

"Let's do a control," the Archaeologist said, and turned it on Trixie. They both eagerly checked her results.

"Ooh!" Trixie purred. "The machine can't get any higher than that."

Magma repeated the scan on Zeke. He looked again, tapped the psychometer and looked a third time.

"Amazing!" he said, waving it under Zeke's nose. The meter was all zeroes.

Zeke sighed. "So there isn't a psychic gene in my body?"

"No, dear boy, you misunderstand. It's off the scale. Your psychic brainwaves are beyond the machine's capacity."

Zeke stared into Magma's arrogant features. Could it really be?

"This explains a lot," Magma said thoughtfully. "Three Mariners activated the Orb of Words before I returned it to Mars. All three died within twenty-four hours, their brains scrambled with Martian syntax and vocabulary. Luckily their dying ravings were enough for Dr Enki, my translator, to master a basic understanding. But you, little blue, opened this Pandora's box and lived. You're formidable, and you never even realised."

Doughty shackled the cage back on. "So Tiberius, we won't need the fat one?"

"Nope. The four in the tent combined with Hailey more than meet our requirements. Take the fat boy to the Happy Hunting Ground."

Scuff paled. "The what?"

Magma gave a cruel smile. "This dig was once a busy one. All manner of experts and interns staffed my camp. Sadly, professional jealousy reared its ugly head. 'You can't do this, you can't do that.' My colleagues kept frustrating my plans with their ethical objections. It became necessary to, um, terminate their contracts. They're all resting now in a nearby gully. Doughty and I call it the Happy Hunting Ground."

"We had some good times up there, eh Tiberius?" Doughty chuckled.

"Wait!" Zeke cried. "You'll need a hostage. Someone to guarantee my obedience."

Magma gave an ice-cold smile.

"You're my prisoner. Prisoners don't bargain, boy."

"Look, I'm new to all this extrasensory business. Scuff's been mentoring me."

"I-I have? No, I mean, I have! He's useless without m-me," Scuff stammered.

Magma looked unconvinced.

"I might be off the scale, but my confidence is less than zero. I've failed every test at the Chasm."

"Is this true?" Magma asked Trixie, who was idly touching up her lipstick.

She snapped her vanity mirror shut and slipped it back into the pocket of her hiking trousers. "Well, Bluey did blow up old Flounder's classroom."

"That's right. My powers either go haywire or totally fail. Scuff can be a stand-in."

Scuff threw Zeke a look that said, 'hey, I'm no stand-in.'

Zeke raised his eyebrows in a reply that meant 'just play along'.

"Hmm, perhaps," Magma replied, stroking his chin. "OK, spare the Canadian for the time being. Regan, fetch the others."

Zeke took a deep, expectant breath. Regan marched out the missing students at gunpoint, all in head cages. First came the tall figures of Jimmy Swallow and Yong Ho Moon, next the portly Hans Kretzmer, and then, at last, Pin-Mei.

"ZEKE!" she cried and broke into a run.

Zeke caught her in his arms and hugged her. Their head cages clanked one against the other.

"I knew you'd save me," she whispered.

"We're in serious trouble, Pin."

"But you'll stop them. I know it."

"Separate!" Doughty barked.

"Come, come," Magma chirped. "I have an appointment with destiny."

Howard prodded Zeke sharply with his gun. Falling into single file they followed Magma into the dark ravines.

Chapter Thirty-Five

The Noctis Labyrinthis

The Labyrinthis was dark and putrid. Magma switched on the torch in his helmet and led the way. The eerie glow revealed twisting, shadowy protrusions of rock, as though clawing monsters had been petrified in a lava flow.

Zeke and the other prisoners followed the professor, stumbling over volcanic shale. Doughty and his men brought up the rear, wearing NVG's. The opaque lenses made them look more insect than human.

Each turn led into a deeper, narrower ravine. A sliver of light far above them was all that remained of the sky. As the gullies closed in Pin-mei tightened her grip on Zeke's arm.

"I'd swear these walls were moving," the normally-rather-sensible Scuff remarked.

"I thought that too. But it's a trick of the light. Right?" It was Jasper Snod, dragging his feet.

"Why are you doing this?" Zeke hissed at him.

"Trixie's making a mint from this—"

"I said you, not Trixie."

"Well, Trixie said it's good for me. She's got big plans for the future. If I play my cards right there'll be a place for me among her deputies."

Zeke cursed. "You came to Mars to become a Mariner. To travel the galaxy. To save the human race. What has Trixie Cutter's nasty little schemes got to do with any of that?"

Jasper opened his mouth to say something, realised he didn't know what to say, and shut it again. He threw Zeke a hateful glare and hurried to the front.

Magma pointed to a seven-foot boulder blocking the trail. "That's it!"

"Why is it so much smoother than the other rocks?" Scuff asked.

"Ah, an observant eye! In different circumstances you'd make an excellent archaeologist."

Scuff muttered something under his breath.

Magma puffed out his chest. "This stone is finely polished and therefore not natural. Evidently the Hesperians placed it here as a marker."

"A marker for what?" Jimmy Swallow asked, a tall handsome boy with chestnut hair.

"The Infinity Trap of course," Magma replied, and squeezed around the boulder.

Doughty tapped Zeke's shoulder with his rifle. "Keep going."

On the other side the gully ran into the mouth of a cave. Without speaking the captives linked hands and braved the blackness. The way was littered with rocky debris and, as they descended, the low roof scraped their heads.

Magma's voice drifted through the void, "Volcanoes and ice carved these caverns when the Earth was just a ball of moltenrock. Hard to imagine, isn't it!"

Suddenly photon lamps flared. They were standing on the threshold of a huge cavern. Clumsy steps led down into a large bowl-shaped floor. A ceiling studded with razor-sharp stalactites arced overhead. Loops of pink and green rock writhed around the periphery, like a nest of petrified serpents. Their coils formed archways into further unlit chambers.

"*Mein Gott!*" Kretzmer gasped.

"You haven't seen anything yet," Magma said. He was standing in the centre of the cavern, beside a small field desk, weighed down with magnopads and various items of equipment. Clearly he'd been working there for months.

"Don't be bashful. Come on down."

He waited impatiently for his audience to catch up.

"It's only fair you kids understand what you're becoming part off. This is one of the most remarkable finds in the solar system. Watch this."

He pulled out a ruby-tinted orb from his rucksack. Zeke sensed at once it was Hesperian, although much smaller than the other orbs, about the size of a large marble. Magma held it aloft on his open palm.

The cavern erupted into life! Thousands of silvery-blue symbols materialised across the rock face, shimmering like glow-worms.

Magma cleared his throat. "This is how I found it. A glittering testament to an extinct race. But what do they mean, all these signs and wonders? Can you understand them, Mr Hailey?"

Zeke examined the twisting basalt surface. "Actually no. It's more like numbers, sums—"

"Theorems and equations is what you mean." Magma gloated. "The linguist Dr Enki and two Nobel winning physicists studied these markings for ages. It's all about quantum decoherence."

"Quantity doo-dummy-whatsit?" Snod asked.

Trixie silenced him with a withering look. "A branch of quantum mechanics that explains there are endless parallel universes, but it is impossible for any of them to connect up."

Swallow and Moon nodded.

"We studied that last term. My brain's still aching," Moon remarked glumly through the bars of his head cage.

Magma bounded over to a portion of the cave wall. "And this bit here show's exactly how to break that rule."

"That's impossible," Moon cried.

Magma laughed. "To our puny science, yes. But the Hesperians found a way round the problem. They captured a slice of infinity, tied it in a loop, and hey presto, an eternal moment!"

"They trapped infinity?" Scuff asked, scratching his brow.

"Yes, exactly. Making a kind of conductor."

"Like those electric conductors on the top of tall buildings, they attract lightening?" Scuff asked again.

Magma nodded enthusiastically. "Except this conducts not electricity but reality. It makes a bridge from here to anywhere."

"A bridge between universes?" Pin-mei ventured, her eyes wide with wonder.

Magma threw his arms in the air. "A bridge between now and any universe, any time, any reality, any consciousness, any damn place you want. Once the Hesperians created it, it had always existed, from the dawn of time till the end of space. And the entrance is located right here at these coordinates. Forever. Even when the Sun goes supernova and swallows Mars up, the doorway will still be here, lost within all that burning plasma."

A pause fell across the party as they took it all in.

"Fascinating for the egghead brigade, but how am I going to turn this into jewellery and real estate?" Cutter asked, checking her make-up in her little mirror.

Magma ran to another part of the cave wall. He indicated a spiral emblem. Zeke shuddered.

"My research proves they also invented a phenomenal power source, which they took through the Trap and stored in a universe alongside ours. Too dangerous to leave lying around Mars. See here." The archaeologist tapped an inscription. "Absorb the Spiral into your mind and you are all-powerful."

"You're wrong!" Zeke shouted. "It says 'the Spiral's power absorbs all minds'."

Regan lifted his rifle but paused when Doughty held up a hand.

"Professor, who's right?"

Magma snorted. "The boy's grasp of Hesperian is useful. But don't be fooled. He's a mere child. These are affairs beyond his mental capacity."

"As long as you're sure," Doughty replied, and nodded to Regan who brought his weapon down on Zeke's spine. He stumbled beneath the blow.

Magma drew himself to his full height, his eyes sparkling like diamonds. "The Spiral is a tool! It allows matter to be controlled by thought. Unlimited amounts of matter. Imagine the Mariner's gift of psychokinesis, but amplified a trillion times. For example, it would enable me to make or unmake things in the blink of an eye. I could create new planets or sweep away old ones. Anything would be possible for me!"

"But how do you access this Spiral?" Doughty interrupted.

Magma underlined the inscription with his finger. "Absorb the Spiral into your mind and you are all-powerful."

Zeke sighed. Magma's scheme for world domination hinged on a mistranslation.

Magma's voice rang aloud. "*Gnthyshi myrythrysraaia dthpzpii !*"

Zeke recognised those words with a chill. 'Awake deathless guardian.' A breeze blew through the mouth of the cave, heavy with sand. It picked up more as it glided into the centre. The ghostly Dust Devil formed before them.

Pin-mei whimpered. Zeke put his arm around her.

"Welcome Caliban!" Magma said with a flourish of his hand.

The creature gave no reply, other than the low moaning of its wind.

"Why do you call him that?" Zeke asked.

"A Shakespearian character, you ignoramus. Caliban was a monstrous servant. Anyway, this is a servant who's been in waiting for two billion years."

"Is it alive?" Trixie asked, stepping towards the whirling figure.

"Define life. I see him more as a robot made from dirt and energy. A creation programmed for obedience. He was out wandering when I happened across this place. Had been for millennia. But sensing the cave was disturbed he returned in minutes. By that time I'd realised the ruby sphere was the cave's control mechanism. I had it in my possession and he has served me ever since."

Trixie waved her hand in front of the creature's blank face. "Does it talk?"

"It mumbles sometimes, in the language of its long dead creators. Too advanced for me, sadly."

"Professor, how do you communicate?" Zeke asked softly.

"By picturing my needs in my head. The creature picks up my thoughts via the ruby sphere."

Zeke's heart leapt. Magma couldn't talk to it directly, the way he could! That gave him a chance, however slender.

"So how do we get in?" Doughty asked.

Magma giggled like a child. He touched a line of text amid the prehistoric calculations. "What does it say, Master Hailey?"

Zeke sighed. "The key is a brain, for thoughts alone unlock the Infinity Trap."

"So kind. Oh, and thank you for translating it in the first place. I could have wasted years trying to figure that one out. It was due to your flare for Martian that I realised I needed to borrow a few quality brains from your revolting school."

"I don't understand," Doughty said.

"The Trap is unlocked simply by thinking," Magma explained, his voice shrill with excitement. "Assuming you have this living tornado's permission, and that your brainwaves are strong enough. Of course, no human brain is. The Hesperians were centuries ahead of us. But the five brightest psychics on Mars, that should do nicely!"

"No way! I'd die before I let you loose on the galaxy," Zeke shouted defiantly.

"Oh dear, that's me finished then," Magma said mockingly. "Men, leave Hailey to last, but shoot the rest of them, beginning with that little piggy."

He waved at Scuff.

Regan and Howard rammed their gun nozzles against Scuff's head and clicked the safety catches.

Chapter Thirty-Six

The Cavern

"**S**TOP!" Zeke roared.

The thugs lowered their weapons.

"Better," Magma said. "The slightest hint of disobedience and the hostage gets it. That was, after all, your idea."

He smiled till he bared his gums. He signalled to Trixie and Doughty. Between them they undid the head cages on everyone except Scuff.

"Now my five little batteries, make a circle here in the centre."

They followed his instructions.

"Now what?" Doughty asked.

"Hmm, I'm not sure." Magma stroked his chin. "I thought the combined brain power of our, um, guests, would do the trick."

"This better not be the wildest goose chase this side of the Asteroid Belt," Doughty snarled, holding his rifle a little higher.

Magma was sweating. With an expression of great reluctance he turned to Zeke. "Ask Caliban. And no tricks."

Zeke looked at the faceless twisting figure. He carefully summoned up the Martian vocabulary.

"*How do we open the Infinity Trap?*"

A mouth appeared in the sand.

"*All think the same. Something good.*"

"*I understand. One more thing. Will you help me? Protect my friend from the Earthmen. If they try to harm him stop them.*"

"*Can I kill them?*"

Zeke hadn't expected that question.

"*Try not to.*"

The creature bowed.

"WHAT! WHAT ARE YOU SAYING?" Magma bellowed.

"Just doing what you said, Professor. Think I've got it."

Zeke took hold of Pin-mei and Jimmy's hands. The rest copied him, forming a chain.

"Who knows the historic London Galactarium? It does a famous show about the sky at night."

Jimmy Swallow nodded.

"Me too," Kretzmer added.

"I've seen the virtual online tour," Pin-mei chirped.

"We have one in Seoul, bigger and better than the London one," Yong Ho said, and managed to grin.

"Good. OK everyone close your eyes and focus on the Galactarium."

Five brows wrinkled in deep concentration.

"Hey!" Snod gasped.

A pair of red swing doors materialised from nowhere.

After a moment of stunned surprise the Lieutenant prowled around them. "They don't go anywhere."

"They do if you go through them," Magma shrieked with exhilaration. "Okay, batteries, I may need you inside. Regan, Howard, stay outside with the fat boy. He's our insurance."

Magma winked very carefully at the goons. He grabbed Pin-mei by the wrist and rushed towards the swing doors. These parted to reveal a dark hole cut clean through reality. The madman and the tiny Chinese girl vanished inside.

Doughty aimed his rifle at Zeke. "You next and no funny stuff. My trigger finger's feeling very itchy."

Zeke needed no encouragement, his fear overshadowed by curiosity. He took a deep breath and dived through the doors.

He was in a familiar place. An ink-blue dome curved overhead, studded with pinpoints of light. A circular floor, filled with rows of seats, sloped down to a fire exit at the bottom.

"Out of the way!" Trixie snapped, shoving him further in.

Zeke studied the artificial night above him, recognising the northern hemisphere in winter. The Twins, the Great Bear, Cassiopeia and Orion were easy to spot. Hanging low in the sky were Orion, Cepheus and Hercules' Club.

"How splendidly old-fashioned. Why did you select this place?" Magma asked.

Before he could answer Magma went on, "I get it! It reminds you of your space-hopping father."

"I used to come here every Saturday. I felt close to—"

"Blah, blah, blah! Okay, Hailey, you're not the only one with a tough childhood. My parents were monsters too."

"My father isn't a monster!"

"Really? He was quick enough to dump you, wasn't he?"

Zeke fell into a crushed silence.

"Is this an illusion?" Doughty asked, scratching his head.

"Not at all, it's totally real." Magma replied in a hushed tone. "Look!"

He took a Martian dollar from his pocket and hurled it at the ceiling. Instead of bouncing off a hard surface the coin kept going, up into space. And yet the light bulb stars seemed near enough to touch. An unpleasant touch of giddiness tickled Zeke at the back of his eyes.

Pin-mei let out a sudden piercing squeal. Two female attendants were approaching up the central aisle. But they were horribly wrong. Each woman's head was a mess of many eyes, noses and mouths.

"They're the usherettes, the women who show you where to sit," Zeke said in a horrified tone. "But they never looked like that!"

"That's what happens when five memories get mixed up." Magma explained, stepping back.

The usherettes wore red uniforms with the Galactarium logo, complete with matching caps. They produced small torches and gestured for the party to follow them to the seating.

"We'll stand, thank you very much," Magma said.

The usherettes walked back a few paces and froze.

"Maybe they sell choc ices in the intermission?" Snod giggled in a very high voice. Nobody noticed.

Professor Magma strode down the main aisle to the midpoint. He fished out the ruby sphere and held it high. He looked back over his shoulder at Zeke and flashed a triumphant smile. "My name is Tiberius Magma. I claim this Infinity Trap as my rightful tool. I demand you take me to the Spiral."

At first nothing seemed to happen.

"Look, the stars are going out!" Zeke gasped.

One by one the glassy sparks faded. As the last one died, they sensed it: a voice speaking to them, only in thoughts rather than sounds.

You are different to the last creatures.

Magma glanced around in astonishment. "Is that the Spiral?"

I am.

"Well, we're not from this planet. We evolved on the third planet and migrated here. The originals are extinct. But surely you know that."

I have slept for aeons.

"Anyway, I am here to claim you. To absorb your power."

Is it safe to return? Has the Age of Comets finished?

"Age of Comets? I don't understand. There is no age of comets."

Magma whispered to Doughty, "It might be a cultural difference."

I must know before I come. Which one of you shall I eat?

No one said anything.

Come now, I hunger.

A small haze appeared low over the western horizon. It rose across the dome to the zenith, expanding. Sure enough it was spiral-shaped. Not a tidy symbol, but a jagged vortex, with smaller spirals sprouting from its thick underside. A bestial mouth salivated at the heart.

I will not visit till I am certain. Nourish me.

"Um, well, why not," Magma replied. There was a tremble in his voice.

"Give it Hailey, give it goodie two shoes," Doughty muttered maliciously.

"Regrettably, we need him. We may need all the batteries. Now let me see."

Magma glanced at Trixie Cutter. Her eyes crackled, full of psychic threat.

"Not you. Ah, that one's the most expendable."

Everyone turned to follow Magma's gaze.

"Hey, why are you all looking at me?" Snod cried.

Doughty swooped down and heaved Snod over his shoulders. He carried the boy, kicking frantically, towards the hideous phenomena.

"PUT ME DOWN! THIS ISN'T FUNNY!" Snod shrieked.

Zeke couldn't bare it. He tore down the aisle. Magma saw him coming and grabbed him tightly.

"TRIXIE! HELP ME! WE'RE MATES!" Snod begged.

Trixie shrugged. "Easy come, easy go Jasper. Success requires sacrifice."

"NOOOOOOOOOOOO!"

With a grunt Doughty heaved Snod up to the brink of the mouth. Zeke tried to break free but Magma's grip was too strong.

Zeke could see the white terror in Snod's face.

The mouth formed lips, lips reaching down from the darkness. Slobbering, the Spiral sucked him up into its folds and the boy's screams were silenced.

Chapter Thirty-Seven

The Infinity Trap

Magma relaxed his grip, quite forgetting Zeke's presence. Zeke backed away as quietly as he could.

"The boy was sufficient." The monster spoke with Jasper Snod's voice, only in a much deeper pitch.

"Ah, you have mastered English. Amazing!" Magma replied, holding himself high. "Now, transfer your power to me."

The Spiral's coils and tentacles shook with laughter. "You don't understand, Professor. I am not a device made by those you call Hesperians. I predate your universe by an eternity."

Magma stamped his foot. "Stop this nonsense. You are a thought-amplifier, a machine for making gods. The invention of the Hesperians."

The tentacles slithered out further from the mouth.

"I remember the Hesperians. They prophesised the Age of Comets, a time of great risk. They were wrong. I've emptied all the contents of Jasper Snod into my belly. Not just his thoughts and genes, but the information stored in his atomic signature. There is no Age of Comets, it must have been a Martian myth and nothing more."

Magma's craggy face turned white. "But we translated the runes!"

"Incorrectly."

There was a terrible pause while Magma and Doughty exchanged feverish looks.

Magma turned back to the Spiral, his eyes gleaming desperately. "Are you hungry for more youngsters? We can lay our hands on a whole school-full of them for you. You can start with these ones, while I go get some more."

The Spiral began rotating slowly. "Yes…hungry. Hungry for EVERYBODY!"

A bang rocked the room. The Spiral rapidly expanded. New offshoots shot across the dome.

Zeke grabbed Pin-mei's hand. "Come on!" He yanked her towards the entrance, where the misshapen usherettes stood shaking like rag dolls. Whack! Zeke ran face first into the doors. They were locked.

The Spiral was taking over.

"I am absorbing the Infinity Trap. This will take a few moments. Please be patient. I will eat you when we are all ready."

The usherettes' multi-eyes melted into spinning spirals. With a tearing noise they ripped in half, making four.

Zeke looked into the terrified faces of the others. He flung his arms around Pin-mei and closed his eyes. There was only one chance now.

Believe, cried his inner voice. *Believe and visualise!*

Zeke imagined his body stepping sideward. Not just his limbs and bones, but every cell. Not just every cell, but the very molecules. Not just the molecules but even the atoms. He pictured electrons tearing themselves from a vibrating chain of energy, sliding and slipping into a different reality. His eyeballs started to glow. Tiny sparks sizzled inside his retinal veins.

He was floating underwater. Floating in outer space. Floating between worlds.

"The cavern. The cavern."

Zeke gasped air into empty lungs. Solid ground supported him. They were back outside!

"You did it!" Pin-mei clapped her hands.

"What's going on?"

It was Scuff peeking from behind a slab of rock.

"Where did the guards go?" Pin-mei asked in a perplexed tone.

"They were going to shoot, Sis. I've never been so scared in all my life. Then abracadabra, that whirly wind thing dragged them from the cave."

"We won't be seeing them again," Zeke said grimly.

He looked through the frosted glass of the Galactarium doors. Lights were flashing.

"Take care of Pin," he said to Scuff.

"You're not going back!" she exclaimed.

Zeke said nothing, summoning his mental energy for another translocation. It was like riding a bicycle, once you knew how to do it, you knew how to do it. He shut his eyes tightly and focused.

When he opened them the Galactarium was rumbling like an earthquake. Doughty had dived into a row of seats and was firing at the Spiral. Magma stood beneath the creature's mouth, too dumbstruck to move. Swallow, Park and Kretzmer were being dragged down the aisle by four usherettes. Trixie Cutter was at the far end rattling the fire exit for all she was worth. Another two usherettes were advancing towards her.

Zeke charged down the aisle and brought his fists down on the back of the nearest usherette. She fell to her knees and Kretzmer broke free from her hold.

"USE YOUR POWERS. TRANSLOCATE!"

"NOT WORKING," Kretzmer shrieked.

Zeke threw himself around the boy. The usherette stood up and stepped towards them. Then nothingness.

"Zeke!" Pin-mei and Scuff cried. The cold dry walls of the cavern surrounded him. Zeke released Kretzmer and vanished.

Inside the Galactarium the Spiral was spinning faster and faster. It was drawing the air up into its huge mouth. A bullet whizzed past Zeke's ear. Doughty had given up on the Spiral and was aiming at the usherettes who were closing in on him. Every one he shot split into two more. Another had pinioned Magma's arms behind his back as he wrestled against her. Trixie Cutter was grappling two of her own and losing the fight.

An usherette stepped out of the group holding the two boys and hurried back towards Zeke. As she was about to capture him he dodged around her. He stretched out his hands.

"HANG ON!"

Swallow and Park reached out. Even as the usherettes hauled the boys closer to the Spiral, Zeke locked his finger with theirs.

The silence of nowhere enveloped him. But this time it was different, this time something was wrong. He was stuck between dimensions. The weight of Swallow and Park was pulling him back to the Galactarium. Translocating himself was one thing, but the mass of two others was too much. The obvious answer was to let go.

"NO!" he grunted, every muscle in his body straining. His eyes crackled brighter than ever.

Think, think, think! Thought is the strongest power in the Universe—in any universe!

Something abruptly gave way. Zeke felt himself falling. With a thud he landed on the stone floor, and a split-second later, the two older boys tumbled on top of him.

"You've done it, bro!" Scuff whooped. "Let's get out of here!"

Zeke sprung up.

Scuff saw the deep frown and burning eyes. He knew that look.

"Zeke no! Those villains aren't worth it. Are you totally nuts?"

"Totally." And he was gone.

He arrived in the Galactarium in the middle of a hurricane. The wind lifted him off the ground. He seized the back of a seat and desperately hung on.

Upside down he surveyed the scene. The air currents were howling around the room before rushing up into the Spiral's mouth. The usherettes stood underneath, as one by one, they jumped and flew up into the orifice. The Spiral no longer needed them, the struggle was nearly over. Magma and Cutter were clinging onto seats too, their bodies flapping like flags. Doughty had wedged himself between the rows, and was weeping.

Magma lost his grip. He flew a few feet before catching Trixie's legs.

"HELP ME"!" he wailed.

Trixie helped him. She kicked him in the chest with every ounce of her strength.

"No-o-o-o." Once. Twice. With the third strike she dislodged him. Screaming uncontrollably Professor Tiberius Magma hurled through the room and up into the Spiral. For a brief moment he lodged in the hole. Then, with a last petrified look at Zeke, he was absorbed.

"If you can do it, so can I," Trixie shouted. Her eyes burned in their sockets. She translocated and was gone.

It was only Zeke and Doughty now. The intensity of the winds increased with every moment.

"SAVE ME! PLEASE!" the Lieutenant sobbed.

There was nothing Zeke could do. There was no way he could overcome the cyclone and reach Doughty. But surely he had to try? His father would want him to do the right thing. Even if it meant never finding him.

"Leopold Doughty, I need you." It was the Spiral.

Doughty's face blanked. He stood up and raised his arms. "Yes, Sir."

Doughty gusted around the Galactarium like a leaf in a wind tunnel. The Spiral snapped him from midair and gobbled him up. Now it turned its attention to Zeke.

"Zeke Hailey, I could show you wonderful things."

"NO!" Zeke bellowed above the storm, clinging to the chair with every ounce of strength.

Translocate now! cried his inner voice.

"Don't you want to see your father?"

Zeke's grip faltered. His dad?

"Let me into your world and I'll take you to him."

"You're lying. He's hundreds of light years away."

"Distance means nothing to me," the Spiral replied casually. "Come, together we will find your father."

"You'll just eat me too!"

"I promise to spare you, and your father. After all, I'll have so many others to enjoy."

Zeke's mind was as chaotic as the howling winds around him. Could it be true?" A dark thrill tingled his spine. A creature as immensely powerful as the Spiral, perhaps this was the only way to reach his father?

Zeke's fingers began to slip. A few more seconds and he would be soaring through the Galactarium, just like the others.

"Your father is in danger, Zeke, but we will save him."

The Spiral's words were as sweet as honey. Zeke ached to believe them.

No, not this way! Better to lose Dad than release this monster!

His hold on the chair gave and he was tumbling through the air.

"NEVERRRRRR!"

Chapter Thirty-Eight

The Cavern again

"**N**EVERRRRRR!"

The blackness between atoms gave way to reality. Zeke was back in the cavern surrounded by his anxious classmates. The Dust Devil was approaching, covering several feet with each stride.

Zeke glanced back at the Galactarium doors.

"Quick, everyone, focus on the doors. Imagine them fading."

The group joined hands.

"Even me?" Scuff asked.

"Especially you," Zeke replied, trying to sound brave.

Their faces contorted as they pictured the doors vanishing. With one eye open Zeke watched the doors turn from solid to transparent. But at the same time he felt an incredible mental energy fight back. Something that dwarfed their intellects the way a planet dwarfs a football. The doors reappeared, warping and distorting like rubber.

Zeke screamed to the Dust Devil in Hesperian, *"We must shut it off."*

The creature moved nearer and stretched out its arms, gesturing to join the circle. Zeke let go of Pin-mei and took the thing's hand. It was like grabbing an electric sander. Pin-mei followed suit. She winced, looked at Zeke then steeled herself.

Six minds from Earth merged with a mind that was alien and ancient. Images and non-human thoughts flooded though Zeke's brain cells. But Zeke ignored them, focusing ever harder on the Galactarium doors.

And quite suddenly the doors were gone.

Zeke stared at the vacant spot. *"Can you tell what is happening inside the Infinity Trap?"*

The living wind cocked its head on one side. *"No."*

"Can it be opened from the inside?"

"No."

Zeke rubbed his chin. *"How can we make sure it never opens again?"*

"Only one way. The Dthpzpii must cease."

Zeke's mouth dropped. *"Why?"*

"The Dthpzpii resonates with the Infinity Trap. Without the shared harmonic connection the Trap cannot engage with this universe."

"How-how can you be ceased?"

"It is simple. By an order from the Old Ones."

Oh that was simple enough. Too bad the Hesperians went extinct two billion years ago.

"You are an Old One."

Zeke recoiled. The creature believed him to be Hesperian because he spoke their language. But to end its life? The responsibility was too much.

The Dust Devil sensed his dilemma. *"The Dthpzpii is not alive. It is a machine."*

"A machine that thinks."

"Less and less with each cycle of the planet. It is corroded. In time it will fail. Remember this. The makers wanted to seal the Infinity Trap."

"So why didn't they?"

"They died too soon."

Zeke thought of all the information that the Dust Devil contained. All the answers it might provide. Then he recalled the look of terror on Snod's face as the Spiral devoured him.

"I'm sorry, I have to give that order."

"Your decision is good. The Dthpzpii is weary."

The Dust Devil began to pick up speed. The humanoid figure inside raised its arms aloft.

"NO! I DIDN'T MEAN NOW!"

The thing spun faster.

"Wait! What did the Spiral mean by the Age of-of—" Zeke desperately searched for the correct Hesperian word.

The Dust Devil was ahead of him. *"Comets,"* it said. *"The Makers prophesised an Age of Comets."*

A blast of dust and air knocked everyone off their feet. Zeke sat up and glanced at five sand-coated faces. The *Dthpzpii* was gone.

They hiked along the bottom of the narrow, winding ravine in silence.

"What was that spiral thing?" Jimmy Swallow asked Zeke at last.

"I've no idea. Something from before the dawn of time."

"There is no 'before' the dawn of time," Scuff insisted.

"So how can we be sure we stopped it?" Swallow went on, wiping his right eye.

"We can't," Zeke said after a pause. He said to Pin-mei, "Was this the premonition you had in Lutz's office?"

She shivered. "It's hard to be sure. Maybe."

"And Magma and the others? Are they dead?" Swallow continued.

Zeke gave him a weird look. "If they're lucky."

Swallow rubbed his eye vigorously. "When that dust creature went ka-boom, a few specks caught in my eye," he said. "Itching like crazy now. Why didn't you warn us it was about to blow up ?"

Yong-Ho Park, walking ahead, swivelled round sharply. "I think Hailey was a little preoccupied with defeating the Spiral. *Kamsamnida*, Mr Zeke, for saving us. Thank you." He shook Zeke's hand forcefully.

"*Ja*, you have the good point," Kretzmer piped up from the rear. He reached out and shook Zeke's hand too. Swallow slowly followed suit, his bad eye blinking and weeping.

"What I want to know is how you managed that feat of translocation," Scuff said.

"Just came to me."

"Yes, but you didn't just shift from one point in space to another. You slipped between parallel universes. That's impossible isn't it?"

Zeke threw his friend an astonished look. "Really? Knimble did say that, didn't he? Must have been the Infinity Trap."

"Maybe it weakened the dimensional walls," Scuff suggested knowingly.

"But when Hans and I tried to translocate nothing happened," Swallow said jealously.

Zeke drew a deep breath. "Cutter got out though. It's just one of those things. Be grateful we're alive."

They were nearing the mouth of the ravine.

"So Fraulein Cutter escaped?" Kretzmer asked.

Still rubbing his eyelid Swallow lifted his head. His one good eye glowed faintly.

"I can see her a few miles off, on the last working scooter." Remote-viewing was his strength. "Practically standing on the accelerator, she is. Got two crocodile skin suitcases."

Zeke grimaced. The orbs! Talk about falling into the wrong hands!

A shaft of light broke the gloom. One by one they stepped out of the shadows and into the fire-red sunset.

"Show me your eye." Pin-mei said to Swallow, gently lowering his arm. It was puffy and sore. "That needs attention."

"There're first aid supplies on Doughty's Bronto. If he left the door open," Scuff remarked.

Swallow swung round. "What do you mean, if it's open?"

"Don't you know anything, the B in Bronto stands for biometric. The machine only works for Doughty. If it's locked, we've had it."

Swallow cursed. "How are we going to get back to the Chasm then?"

"Good question," Zeke said, and began walking towards the dilapidated tents.

Fortunately the Bronto was open. Pin-mei dabbed Swallow's injury with antiseptic. The others scoured the camp. Swallow was right about the scooters, they were all broken. There were no rescue beacons or anything else of use. The food supplies were enough to last three days and no more.

"Can't you hack into the Bronto's mainframe?" Zeke asked Scuff.

"Not without a separate memory file, like Albie for example. Too bad he went up in flames."

The last embers of daylight flared in Zeke's deep dark eyes. He dived into the Bronto and jumped out brandishing his backpack.

"What makes you think I'd leave Albie behind?" he cried happily, and fished out the silvery disc.

"Now we're cooking, bro!"

Scuff grabbed Albie, disappearing inside the black hull.

"Pin, I nearly forgot," Zeke said, rummaging through his pack. He pulled out a leather bound journal.

"The Beagle Research Station?" Pin-mei replied in a puzzled tone.

"Not that. This!"

Out came a grubby Mr Raffles.

"Goodness!" she exclaimed. "You brought him all this way for me?"

"Through thick and thin, he's survived crash, fire, and blizzard!"

Pin-mei hugged her teddy. Then she hugged Zeke.

"Thank you to the power of a zillion, Zeke. You saved me. I knew you would."

Zeke's face turned cherry red. He wanted to say something, but the words wouldn't come.

"Zeke, there's been something I've been meaning to ask you," Pin-mei said suddenly, with a sheepish look.

Zeke nodded for her to go on.

"Did your mother really drop a cartridge of nano-ink on your head?"

Zeke laughed out loud. He laughed like he hadn't laughed in weeks. "Of course not, Pin, that's Mum's little joke! Blue hair is in my family's genes. You know, like albinos are white. My Dad's the same."

"Oh, I see," Pin replied, with a look that said she was none the wiser.

The Bronto engines roared into life.

"That was quick," Pin-mei observed.

"Scuff might be a clumsy psychic," Zeke said. "but he's a wiz at computers."

Buzzing with excitement everyone crowded onto the bridge. Scuff was looking rather pleased with himself. He puffed out his chest and said, "We'll be in Tithonium Central in two days. We can buy fresh provisions and tell the authorities what happened. If we don't get locked in a mental hospital it will be another three days to the Chasm."

A volley of cheers resounded through the vehicle.

Scuff turned to the console. "Albie, full steam ahead."

"Voice analysis indicates you are not Zeke Hailey."

Scuff rolled his eyes.

"Full steam ahead, Albie," Zeke said obligingly.

"Affirmative, Master."

The steel flooring shuddered. They were moving!

"*Annyongi Kaseyo*. Good bye and good riddance," Park said, peeking through the window at the dark shapes of Magma's camp.

"I want top bunk," Kretzmer chuckled.

With a chorus of squeals and hoots Kretzmer, Swallow, Park, and Pin-mei bolted for the doorway. Zeke and Scuff sat down at the controls. Scuff produced a couple of cans of Craterade, and passed one to his friend. They pulled the rings and took a long sip.

"We're not having much luck finding your father, Zeke."

"Well I did get rather sidetracked. But I can make it my number one priority, and thanks to you, I have a lead now. The Flying Dutchman Project."

"When we get back to school we can start combing the place for clues."

"We've been expelled, remember," Zeke said ruefully.

Scuff smirked. "As soon as the others tell their story, our names will be cleared. More than that, we'll be heroes. Lutz will have to reinstate us."

"Even me, the school fake?"

"Especially you, Zeke. You're psychic now."

"So I am!" Zeke said happily.

"That makes you the School's responsibility."

Zeke thought for a moment "We could go and work for Ptolemy Cusp, if only to get Justice off the hook."

"He can look after himself, " Scuff replied. "Where else but the School can you study telepathy, precognition, translocation, etcetera, all the skills you're going to need to track down your old man."

"Where else indeed," Zeke agreed.

"Anyway, those freetowners were a rum lot. I didn't like the way that Isla woman badmouthed the Mariners."

"She had a point though. Why don't the colony ships ever return?"

Scuff snorted. "Baloney. The colonists are too busy. Obviously!"

"And my dad?" Zeke asked sharply.

"Well, he's the exception."

Zeke drew in a long deep breath. "You know, Scuff, I have this feeling something's going on. Something big. And the Mariners know all about it. Even Lutz. Maybe my father was trying to get to the bottom of it. He was on a secret mission, after all."

"Well if that's the case, bro, all the more reason to become a Mariner."

"Huh?"

"It's the best possible place to find out what's going on."

"You're right, " Zeke said, folding his arms. "It's the Ophir Chasma School for me."

Zeke's face, lit by the glow from the computers, formed a pale oval in the dark of the Martian night. He was grinning his lopsided grin as he looked out, up to the brilliant stars.

"He might be light years away, but I've taken the first step. I'm going to find him, Scuff. From Orion to Andromeda, whatever corner of the galaxy he's in, I'm going to find my dad. "

Mars is a planet of secrets. Uncover the truth at Zeke's web site: www.zekehailey.com

Find out who among Zeke's friends has something to hide. Learn fun facts about Mars. Connect with author Ian C Douglas and share your thoughts on the book. And, most of all, get exclusive previews to *Gravity's Eye*, Zeke's next thrilling adventure.

Lightning Source UK Ltd.
Milton Keynes UK
UKOW04f1650221213

223503UK00001B/23/P